Secret Sisters #1

**Book One:
Heart to Heart**

**Book Two:
Twenty-One Ponies**

Sandra Byrd

www.sandrabyrd.com

Secret Sisters:(se'-krit sis'-terz) n. Two friends who choose each other to be everything a real sister should be: loyal and loving. They share with and help each other no matter what!

Secret Sisters

Book One:
Heart to Heart

Sandra Byrd

It looks like Tess may lose her best friend! Will sixth grade be the worst year of her life?

Tess gasped as she faced the mirror. The simple circle she had drawn on it yesterday had now been transformed into a complete face with crossed eyes and a crooked mouth. Worst of all were the huge ears with the word "Dumbo" written in one and "Flyers" in the other. Underneath someone had scrawled, "Mirror, Mirror, on the wall, who's the biggest geek of all? Tess Thomas!"

Tess turned around and grasped for a stall. The ceiling circled the stall as if in orbit, and she couldn't get a deep breath. She rested on the toilet seat. After a few minutes, the room slowed down, but hot tears still splashed her cheeks. Unlike yesterday, Tess couldn't will herself not to cry.

The Coronado Club, of course! But which one drew this? Lauren? Andrea?

Then she remembered. The only person who had heard her called "Dumbo Flyers" last summer was Colleen. Tess couldn't believe it. Not Colleen! Just a few weeks ago, Tess would have defended her friend to anyone, certain Colleen would have done the same for her.

Now Colleen had turned on her.

Chapter One
There Must Be Some Mistake

Friday, August 30

The Arizona heat shimmered above the sandy desert landscape. Hot asphalt squished beneath Tess's sandals as she and her best friend, Colleen, raced up the last hill before reaching school. Today was posting day at Coronado Elementary, the day they would find out whose classes they were in.

"Everybody's crowding the hallways!" Tess pushed her long chestnut hair back as she headed toward the sixth-grade hall.

"I know, the little kids came with their mommies," Colleen said. "I'm glad we're old enough to come alone."

She could still hear Colleen, but Tess's attention was drawn away. A young girl with pink-ribbon pigtails plopped to the floor, having been tripped by some eager kid racing down the main hall. "Here, let me help." Tess grabbed the girl's elbow and pulled her to her feet. The girl smiled, and then her mother came forward, clasping her daughter with relief. That taken care of, Tess scanned the hall for her friend.

There she was, over by last year's class pictures.

"Hey, speed up!" Colleen called as Tess hurried toward her. "Look at my hair last year. Ick. It's better with bangs, don't you think? I can't wait until they take new pictures and toss these in the trash."

Tess was about to say how nice Colleen's hair had looked last year, too, but Colleen kept right on talking. "Come on, let's hit the lists! I wonder who else is in our class." They continued down the hall toward the sixth-grade rooms, but Tess couldn't avoid glancing at her fifth-grade class picture. Her smile wilted as her eyes drew to the lonely girl standing on the edge of the crowd, hands behind her back, face downcast.

"There I am," she whispered to herself. Tears welled as she remembered the solitary lunches, reading alone at recess, watching other girls pass notes while she pretended to do her work. Worst of all, no one had ever chosen her to be science partner, and science was her best subject. Being the new girl had been hard. She'd ended up mismatched with other leftover kids.

"Oh, well, not this year." She blinked the moisture from her eyes and caught up with Colleen.

Nerves buzzed Tess's stomach as they approached the classroom doors. "I hope we're together."

"We will be," Colleen said. "My mom called the school to make sure I was assigned to Mr. Basil. Last year his class won the math decathlon."

"I heard that Mr. Basil doesn't read notes aloud if he catches you passing any or confiscate your phone," Tess added. She reached his door first and scanned the list, the list that would make her day or doom her life.

"Here's your name, Colleen Clark. Right at the top with the other C's."

"Yes!" Colleen said, giving Tess the thumbs up. "Check for your name."

"Terrence, Albert," Tess read aloud. "Tongue, James." She stopped, unwilling to believe what she saw. Or didn't see. She checked the list again. "You're kidding. No way! I'm not in this class?" Thomas, Tess did not appear on the list.

"It's okay." Colleen circled her arm around her friend's shoulders. "Don't worry. Maybe they made a mistake. Maybe your name isn't on any list. Come on, let's check the other rooms."

Tugging on Tess's arm, Colleen dragged her to the next classroom, Ms. Froget's. Nobody wanted "The Frog." Her breath was heavy with menthol cigarettes, and she handed out pink discipline slips like reverse Valentines. She delivered at least one to each student, more to those kids she didn't really like.

"Thank goodness," sighed Tess, hastily reading the list. "No Thomases. Maybe there is a mistake." Her stomach calmed, and her heart filled with hope. She would be in Colleen's class after all.

"See, I told you we would be together. We have to," Colleen said. "Next, Ms. Martinez's room." They marched toward the last sixth-grade classroom. "You can have your mom call the school and explain that your name was left off Mr. Basil's list." Colleen reached Ms. Martinez's door first and started to read the names.

"Oh, no," she groaned. "Your name is here. This is totally bad!"

Tess gulped air before diving through the list. Sure enough, there was her name. She searched for anyone else she knew.

No one.

"Don't worry. I have a plan," Colleen said.

Colleen always did. She was pretty and popular, and Tess could hardly believe her good luck when Colleen had picked her out of all the other girls on the swim team to pal up with over summer. Colleen knew everybody, and Tess hoped she would finally be popular, too.

"Go home and tell your mom to call the school," Colleen instructed. "She can insist that you have to be in Mr. Basil's class. They're pretty good about changing teachers if parents call. We need to be in the same class!"

"I know," Tess said. "But I don't know if my mom will call."

"Explain to her how important it is. Does she know how depressed you'll be if we're not together? Does she want you to be alone? Besides, I've been thinking we should start a club, and we have to be together for that!" Colleen stared into the window of Ms. Martinez's door, using it as a mirror. Grabbing half of her ponytail in each hand she pulled it tight, then she poofed her bangs.

"You're right...," Tess mumbled.

Colleen spun around and cried out, "Lauren, you're back! How fabulous."

Tess snapped out of her daze.

"Hi." Lauren Mayfield ran up and hugged Colleen. "I'm in Mr. Basil's class, and I saw your name on the list, too! Isn't that cool?"

"Yes!" Colleen answered.

"Are you in Mr. Basil's class?" Lauren turned toward Tess.

Colleen answered for her. "No, she isn't. I mean, not yet, anyway. Her mom's going to get her in."

"Great," Lauren said, but not as if she meant it. She looked at Tess again with a prize-winning, fake smile. Tess faked a smile back at her. Unlike Tess, Colleen had had a best friend in fifth grade—Lauren. However, Lauren had been away at her grandparents' farm for most of the summer and hadn't been sure if she was coming back. At least, that's what Colleen had thought. Looking at them together, Tess had the uneasy feeling that Lauren was back in more ways than one.

Lauren turned to Colleen. "Do you want to come over to swim?"

"Sure," Colleen answered. "Let's run to my house and pick up my bikini." She turned toward Tess and continued, "You can come, too, if you want."

"Yeah, um, sure," Lauren muttered.

"No, thanks," Tess said. She could tell Lauren

5

didn't want her there. "I told my mom I'd come right home, and I need to talk to her about calling the school."

"Right. Good idea." Lauren grabbed Colleen's arm to pull her down the hall toward the front door. "Let's go! It's getting late."

"Bye, Tess. I'll call you later," Colleen promised over her shoulder as she started down the hall. Tess stood there, watching them leave. Lauren whispered something in Colleen's ear, and they both giggled.

At that moment Tess knew, she just knew, they were walking away from her forever.

Chapter Two
First Morning

Tuesday, September 3

The alarm announced Tuesday morning much too soon. When it bleated at 7:00 A.M., Tess begged for five more minutes. She struggled to force her eyes open but then gave up and dozed off again.

A few minutes later a faint tapping noise awakened her as Mrs. Thomas opened the door and poked in her head. "Time to wake up, honey. I made a special breakfast. Come and eat before Tyler finishes it off." She gently shut the door.

Pushing her hair away from her face, Tess reached her hands toward the ceiling, stretched, and then slid out of bed. Oh, yeah. How could she have forgotten? The first awful day of sixth grade.

Fifteen minutes later three outfits were inside out and thrown about the room, discarded like fashion roadkill as quickly as they had been considered. The outfit she had chosen last night didn't seem right today. She wanted to wear something that would show off her "Forever Friends" necklace, the one Colleen had given her last summer. Just in case Lauren has any doubts about who is Colleen's best friend now.

Tess went back to the dresser and yanked out the baby blue T-shirt she had purchased yesterday at Robinson's-May. After pulling it on, she smoothed her hand over her static-filled hair. "There. I guess this looks okay. I wonder what Colleen will wear." Probably something blue, too, since that was Colleen's favorite color.

Tinny music twanged, and the faithful ballerina twirled in Tess's jewelry box while she sorted through the tangled mess. Finally finding the hidden dangling earrings, she put them on. Dangling earrings were forbidden by her mom, but maybe that rule was for last year. Surely sixth grade was different. After retrieving a necklace from under her shirt, she abandoned the clutter to walk to the bathroom.

"Disgusting! Is it asking too much for Tyler to rinse out the sink after brushing his teeth?" She stared at globs of toothpaste, just like every other morning. The mornings Tyler remembered to brush his teeth, that is. How could a kid who polished his sneakers leave this mess? She ran the hot water hard, hoping the goop would wash down. It didn't, sticking, instead, like stubborn green worms on the white porcelain. She squeezed some mint gel on her toothbrush and, after brushing, washed her face. Then she switched off the bathroom light and headed out the door.

"Wait a second!" Flicking the light back on she

remembered. Lip gloss. Breaking open a new tube of Passion Fruit, she let it glide over her lips. Mmm. She kissed the mirror, leaving a slightly sticky smooch on its smooth surface. Perfect.

A minute later she slipped into her chair at the breakfast table and sipped her milk. Mrs. Thomas set a plate of fresh pancakes in front of her. They were a pleasant change from the usual yogurt. Steam rose, thickly scenting the air with plump, hot blueberries squeezed into a buttermilk robe. Tess's stomach meowed. Maybe she felt hungry after all.

"There's still time, you know," Tess started.

"Time for what, honey?" Her mom flipped a stack onto her own plate and sat down.

"To call the school. And change my class."

"Tess, we've already been over this. You were assigned to Ms. Martinez's class. She might be really nice. We don't know anything about her. Besides, I'm sure you'll make some new friends; maybe you'll even like them as much as Colleen. Try to have a positive attitude. Sulking isn't going to help." She finished her sentence and took a bite.

Tess's face fell. Didn't her mom understand? Not if she could say things like "positive attitude."

Fear and anxiety bubbled until Tess burst out, "I am positive I'm not changing any attitude until you call the school!" Her lips quivered.

"Watch your tone, Miss," Mom said.

"You don't understand. You're ruining my life!" Tess stood back from the table.

Tyler glanced up from his meal. "Girls. Never

9

could understand them. Glad I don't have to." He plucked a cricket from an old margarine container hidden on the floor and lifted the top off his horned toad's cage, dropping the tasty tidbit in. Hercules gobbled it up. "No need for you to go hungry, old boy," Tyler said, mimicking the accent he heard on the British mystery television shows he watched.

Sickened by the bug's death on top of everything else, Tess fled the room, running down the hall to her bedroom. Once she was in her room, she flopped onto her bed. How could she face this day? This year? She heard a light knock on her door. She sat there for a moment, glancing at the clock before answering. Her clock glared "7:45" at her in bold red numerals.

"Yes?"

"Come on, honey. I do understand. And I'll give you a ride so you won't be late." Mom's steps softened as she pattered back down the hall.

"Maybe it won't be so bad," Tess said to her reflection, slowly straightening her shirt in front of her full-length mirror. "Maybe Lauren will find another friend." Grabbing her backpack, she was off to join her mom and Ty in the car.

"Hey, I thought it was my turn to pick the music." Tess opened one of the back doors. She climbed in and buckled up as Tyler turned to face her.

"Too bad, you lose," he said, forming the letter L with his thumb and fingers and placing it against his forehead to signal "Loser."

Impossible, Tess thought, rolling her eyes, to live with an eight-year-old boy. I'd much rather have had a sister.

Scrunch. The bottom of the car scraped the sidewalk. Her mom always backed out too fast. Two minutes later they swooped into the school parking lot, a lone eagle landing among flocks of hawks.

The car lurched as Mrs. Thomas pulled in and then slammed on the brakes. Tess crouched down in her seat, hoping no one saw the car screech to a humiliating halt. She sat up as Tyler bounded out of the car.

Her mom cleared her throat and held out her hand toward Tess.

"What?" Tess asked.

"The earrings. They dangle."

"Oh, Mom, come on." Even as Tess said it, she unclasped the earrings, handing them to her mother. Obviously, her mom didn't think being in sixth grade made any difference. Dutifully, Tess brushed a kiss on her mother's cheek and turned to go.

"I love you, Tess," her mom called after her. "Make it a great day."

Sandra Byrd

Chapter Three
New Year, Old Feelings

Tuesday, September 3

The motto YOU ARE BECOMING WHO YOU ARE TO BE was engraved in smooth stone above the main door to the stuccoed school. Tess stared at it for a minute before heading toward the sixth-grade hallway, hanging around to see if she could catch Colleen. After a few minutes had passed with no sign of her friend, she slouched into class.

She was one of the first to arrive. As she put away her supplies, she heard someone ask, "Is anyone sitting here?"

Tess looked up at a girl with French-braided hair the color of light caramel syrup. The girl motioned toward the desk next to Tess.

"No, uh, I don't think so," Tess answered. The girl set her backpack on the desk and opened it up. Tess finished arranging her things and zipped her backpack shut.

A tube of the girl's lip gloss dropped to the floor, and she bent over to retrieve it. "What flavor is that?" Tess blurted before she could stop herself.

13

"Mango. This is the first year I can wear any kind of makeup to school," the girl answered. She didn't seem to mind the question. "I really like the scent. It reminds me of the trip we took to Hawaii last year." When the girl smiled, her whole face looked happy, not just her mouth. Cool. Real. Not faked, like Lauren's.

Tess said, "This is the first year I can wear lip gloss to school, too. Mine's Passion Fruit." She glanced at a picture the girl had set a picture on the top of her desk. "Is that your horse?"

"Yeah, I have two horses. I mean, my grandparents have horses at their house in Gilbert. They seem like my horses, though, because I like them better than anyone else does. I mostly ride the two youngest, Dustbuster and Solomon."

"I like horses. Only I don't get to ride much. My mom took me to Tapatio Stables once."

An awkward moment passed before the girl smiled at Tess again, then turned back to her desk.

The first bell rang, signaling Ms. Martinez to call the class to order. She was young. And she had a 3-D solar system model in the science corner. This might be okay.

"My name is Erin," the girl across the aisle whispered before turning away to talk with others.

"My name is Tess," she replied softly to Erin's back as Ms. Martinez gave her opening introduction. The Pledge of Allegiance crackled on the intercom, and the school year began.

An hour later Tess decided she needed a drink of

water. On the way, she would peek into Mr. Basil's class to get Colleen's attention. Maybe Colleen could get a drink, too, and the two of them could make a plan to meet at recess and lunch. Once in the hall, Tess buzzed directly to Mr. Basil's class.

His back was turned, and as Tess scanned the class, her eyes rested uncomfortably on a group surrounding Colleen...and Lauren. With their desks side by side, they looked a little too cozy. After a moment of longing, Tess returned to her classroom, forgetting about the drink of water. She would have to do something about this. This year was not going to be the fifth grade all over again.

Sandra Byrd

 Chapter Four
Squaw Peak

Thursday, September 5

Two nights later was hiking night, a special time almost every week when Tess and her dad were together. As usual, her father reached the top of Squaw Peak first. Like the chubby finger of a demanding baby, Squaw Peak jutted out from the mostly flat palm of the Phoenix landscape. From a distance, the mountain looked smooth and steep. Close up, though, crumbling rocks, cracks, crevices, and the beaten path from thousands of hikers who climbed this trail each year came into focus.

Tess's dad chose a smooth rock to sit down on before taking off his glasses. Pulling a small towel out of his fanny pack, he wiped the sweat from his glasses and then from his forehead before putting the glasses back on. Tess sat down next to him and guzzled a long drink from her water bottle.

In fact, Tess and her dad had climbed this trail dozens of times. He felt exercise was good for the soul and built a competitive spirit; so he made sure the family got plenty of it. Tess loved hiking and usually her father's company. Most of all she enjoyed the watercolor sunset as dusk filtered through layers of desert dust. Evening light bathed the mountain, warming the stubborn little shrubs clinging to its nooks and crannies.

"What's up?" Her dad broke the silence.

"What do you mean?"

"Well, Mom says you've been sassy the last few days, short-tempered. That's not like you. You're usually a defender of the downtrodden, sunshine for the sad-hearted."

"Dad...," Tess rolled her eyes at the exaggeration. Sometimes she felt uncomfortable talking about her private thoughts, especially with her dad. But worry about school boiled over, spilling out in words. "I feel totally left out. I finally have a best friend and a really good chance to be in the popular group. But now, since I'm not in Colleen's class, I'm afraid I won't have any friends at all!" Her face flushed with heat and embarrassment.

Her dad clasped her shoulder. "I'm sorry to hear it." Tess could tell by the look on his face that he didn't get it. "I'm sure you'll be okay. You're strong. You'll make some new friends. Quit worrying about it; do something! There's always hope, even when things seem darkest. Remember," he said as he stood up, motioning for her to start down the trail, "it's not always about getting the best situations, instead—"

"Do the best you can with the situation you have."

Tess finished the thought with a sigh. She had heard that line at least sixty-six times.

What did he expect her to do with this situation? Maybe he could just brush it off, but Tess couldn't. Her dad meant well; yet he obviously didn't understand how major it was to have friends. Popular friends. Any friends, actually, besides the ones at her old school, whom she hardly ever talked to anymore.

It had been more than a year since she had moved. Her parents had thought moving would be a good thing—nice schools and close to everything. But it hadn't worked out that way for Tess.

Until Colleen, that is. Colleen had included her in everything, introducing her to important people. It was a miracle they had met on swim team. How lucky Tess was to be picked by Colleen. Colleen cared about Tess. What was her dad thinking? What should she hope for?

"Now that we have that settled, I hope you'll be civil to your mother. Okay?" Her father waited for an answer, and after Tess nodded in agreement, he turned back toward the trail.

It wasn't really settled, but her heart ached at the possibility that she had hurt her mom's feelings. Her mother could get on her nerves, but Tess loved her. She was the best mother around. Tess promised herself she would do better. She hated to hurt anyone's feelings; she knew how that felt.

"Hey, Dad," Tess called as she scooted past him. She raced a few steps ahead on the trail before calling over her shoulder, "Last one to the car is a brown banana. Do I need to remind you who was the brown banana last week?"

He chuckled, stepping up his pace a little too late.

🌵

"What are you doing in here?" Tess tossed her shoes into the closet as she stepped into her room.

"Mom said I could use your computer to finish my homework. I wish I had one of my own." The computer beeped as Tyler exited through a myriad of screens to close down his work.

"Yeah, well, maybe next year. I had to wait until Mom bought a new one for work. Next time she buys one, you can have this, and I'll take the one she has now."

"You stink," Tyler said. "I really mean it, old girl. Stinkus amongus. Perhaps you should visit the W.C. and tidy up."

"Can you lay off that English accent? And what is Hercules doing in here?" Tess tapped the side of the toad's cage. She might be more favorably inclined toward Hercules if he weren't always devouring helpless bugs.

"Mom was banging around in the kitchen tonight, and he got scared and shot blood at her through his eyes. It hit the glass, but Mom got mad and said he had to stay out of the kitchen. So he'll bunk with me from now on." Tyler grabbed the cage on the way to his room.

"Nice. You can have blood on your walls then."

Tess pulled out her phone and clicked on her "Hidden Treasures" app.

Dear Diary,

I'm worried this may be the worst year of my life. I am not kidding or exaggerating. This is supposed to be my best grade, the one in which I am a boss of the school before I start middle school, but too bad for me. Everyone I know is in Mr. Basil's class, except for one girl I just met. She, Erin I mean, is okay, but she's not Colleen. Don't you think I deserve to have friends, Diary? I've worked hard to be popular. Lauren is trying to take Colleen away from me. I just know it. The worst part is I have no one to talk to except a stupid diary. No offense. Mom would never understand. She would tell me, "Make new friends and keep the old. One is silver and the other's gold" or something else silly.

I tried to talk with Dad tonight, but it went right over his head. He always thinks it will be okay. He says there's hope, but what hope could there be?

Hey! I just remembered the club, the club that Colleen said we're going to start. If we start it right away, we can get totally involved in that together! I'll remind her of it tomorrow. Maybe Dad's right. Maybe hope is coming. I wish you were real, Diary. I wish you could talk and help me, tell me what to do. But of course you can't. Good night, Diary.

Love, Tess

PS. Ms. Martinez seems pretty good so far. I'll give you an update later.

 Chapter Five
Coronado Club

Friday, September 6

Tess fidgeted, trying to pass the time until lunch so she could get Colleen by herself and talk about starting the club. "Sixth graders, please return to your seats," Ms. Martinez instructed at the end of free time. Except for the clock's loud ticking, the room grew quiet.

"The district is sponsoring a science contest, open to every sixth-grade class in Scottsdale," Ms. Martinez continued. "The winning class will earn a field trip to the planetarium in Tucson with a lunch stop at McDonald's. I love the planetarium, so I want us to win! Your first assignment is to write a proposal on what you think the class should submit as our project. Submissions are due in one week. I'll review them all before choosing one. The class will work together on the project, and we'll turn it in by the end of October. The winning class will be announced right before Thanksgiving. I'm sure we can win, if we work hard. After all, we are the smartest class, right?" Ms. Martinez winked. "I'll give final instructions after lunch."

She returned to the board, erasing the last lesson before writing out math problems. Chalk dust floated through the air, and the escaping powder tickled Tess's nose.

From her seat next to Tess, Erin passed a note. "Have you ever been to the planetarium? Circle one: Yes, No"

Tess slid down behind her desk so she could read the note without being seen. She circled "No," then wrote: "It sounds fun. A day without school sounds fun, too. So does lunch at McDonald's. I hope we win. I like your hair braided that way. Do you do it yourself?"

She dropped the note on the floor between their desks. Erin reached down to pick it up and returned: "Yes. I can do yours, too, if you want. It would look great."

"No thanks," wrote Tess. She chewed her pencil eraser for a minute before adding, "I don't pull my hair back." She didn't explain that at the Y swim team this past summer a boy had taken one look at her ears and called them "Dumbo Flyers." Everyone, absolutely everyone, laughed. Even Colleen. Afterward, Tess vowed she would never pull her hair back again. She held the note under her palm, securing it with her thumb, and slipped it back. Ms. Martinez looked up with a stern expression, as if to say "No more notes" just before the lunch bell rang.

Kangaroo meat again. At least the rumor said it was kangaroo meat chopped up inside the stroganoff.

That's sure what it smelled like. Tess watched as the lunchroom workers slopped food onto her neon tray that was beat up enough to have been here since Colonel Scott founded the city. At least the fries looked good, and the salad did, too. Tess waited in line with the others for dessert, grabbing some silverware and a carton of skim milk.

Colleen strode in, and the kid behind Tess let Colleen cut in. "Hi, how's old Martinez doing?"

"Not bad," Tess answered, smiling. "And she's not old. She just graduated from college."

"Oh," said Colleen, looking around. "Well, what I really came to tell you is that I started the club. It's called the Coronado Club. It's only for cool sixth graders. Like you, of course. Lauren's already in. I talked to her yesterday. We can't wait for you to be a member, too."

"Great," Tess said, perking up. She wasn't going to be left out after all. "It's so amazing how we think alike! I was going to ask you about the club today. Why don't you tell me more at the table?"

"Well," Colleen shifted her weight between her feet, staring at the ground. "That's the problem. We decided our table would only be for active club members. You're going to be a member, of course, after you're initiated. But you're not a member yet; so you can't sit with us today."

"What do you mean, initiated? You're my best friend!"

"I know, but each member has to do something

important to prove her loyalty to the others," Colleen insisted, looking Tess in the eye. "Of course, we know you're loyal. It won't be a problem. I'll talk to the others today and ask them what your initiation will be. I'll text you over the weekend, okay?"

"Well, I guess so," Tess answered, even though it wasn't. "I thought maybe we could do something together this weekend."

"I'm sorry. I already have plans. Maybe next weekend? I'll call you Sunday." Colleen squeezed Tess's arm, then cut out of line, walking back to stand with Lauren.

Tess walked through the lunchroom, finally sitting down at a table toward the middle. *Prove my loyalty to whom? What is going on? Colleen never left Tess out. Tess needed Colleen, and Colleen needed Tess. Right?* She glanced over at the table where Colleen and Lauren sat. Melody Shirowsky sat with them, pushing her sleeves up her long, slender arms and flashing her dimpled smile. Everyone thought Melody was the prettiest girl in sixth grade. Tess wondered if Melody had to be initiated or if she was cute enough to be in automatically.

"Hey, are you alone? Can I sit here?"

Tess looked up to see it was Erin.

"Sure," she answered, still upset. "Go ahead." She wondered if Erin thought it was weird that Tess sat alone. Erin must have noticed Tess usually sat with Colleen. Tess hoped people wouldn't think she was a nerd or anything.

"I brought some more pictures of my horses. Oh, I mean my grandparents' horses. I wondered if you want to see them." Erin pulled out an envelope thick with pictures.

"Okay."

Erin unstuck the envelope and handed the photos over one by one. "This one is Dustbuster. Whenever she runs, she kicks up a lot of dust. She's a quarter horse with a really good personality. She loves carrots. And guess what? She'll only eat them if they've been peeled!" Erin giggled as she passed the next picture along. Tess's anger was forgotten for now, and she giggled back.

"This one is named Solomon because he is wise. He can tell if his rider is new or experienced. He is gentle with an inexperienced rider but gives a trained rider a wild ride." Erin passed across a few more photos. Tess noticed a cute boy in one but was too embarrassed to ask who he was.

"These are so cool, Erin. Thanks for showing me." Tess finished her lunch and asked, "Where's Jessica?" Erin usually sat with Jessica Blessing, her best friend, who was in The Frog's class.

"In Seattle for a couple of days."

"Do you want to go outside?" Tess asked. She figured that was better than sitting in the lunchroom alone.

"Okay." Erin crumpled her napkin into a ball and piled the rest of her trash onto the tray. "Let's go."

Tess followed her to the garbage can where they cleared their trays. The usually noisy lunchroom was quiet. Almost everyone had escaped into the hot noon sunshine. Tess wondered what Colleen would think of Erin and whether Colleen liked horses.

Funny, even though Colleen was Tess's best friend, Tess didn't know a lot about her.

Chapter Six
Initiation

Sunday, September 8

After a boring weekend of yard work with "General Dad" giving orders and no help from lazy "Lieutenant Tyler," Tess couldn't wait for Colleen's text. It finally came.

"I bought a new outfit." Colleen's text said.

"Really?" Tess texted back. "What's it like?"

"It's a black sweater dress with a jazzy black velvet hat. Also, I bought some new Cheri shampoo, the kind that washes a tint into your hair. I finally convinced my mom I'm old enough to try it. Oh, yeah, I'll bring your book back to school this week. Thanks for loaning it to me."

"No problem," Tess texted back. She sat on the floor folding a big pile of her clothes while she talked. "Where did you buy the shampoo?"

"At Pay Less-Save More," Colleen answered. "That reminds me. Your mom almost ran over my mom in the parking lot last week. I heard my mom tell my dad that Molly Thomas needs driving lessons before she kills someone."

A hot flush rose from Tess's neck to her forehead, prickling her hair. Colleen's mom, of all people.

"Sorry," Tess responded. "Tyler was probably distracting her." Tess moved on to another stack of clothes but kept her phone near.

Colleen continued. "I talked with the other club members, and we've decided on your initiation."

Tess stopped one-hand folding clothes and held her phone with both hands; a funny tingle danced in her stomach.

"The club has decided that for your initiation you have to trip Unibrow as she takes her tray to her lunch table this Friday."

"What do you mean?" Tess texted. "Who's Unibrow?"

"You mean you don't know who Unibrow is? You're out of it, Tess. I can see I'm going to have to clue you in. Do you know Marcia Porcetti?"

"Yeah, I think so. Is she Unibrow?"

"Yes," Colleen confirmed with one long text that spilled onto several pages one after another. "Haven't you noticed her eyebrows? She's so hairy her eyebrows practically connect. It's disgusting. You can't tell where one brow begins and the other ends. So she's a unibrow. And her arms are hairy, too. She's like an ape. Anyway, she's always one of the last people into the lunchroom. Here's the plan. Friday sit at the very end of the table. Then, when Marcia walks by, stick out your foot and trip her. Everyone will laugh hysterically. Okay?"

Now Tess's stomach was a big blob of playdough

that was being squeezed, punched, and kneaded. "I don't even know Marcia," Tess replied. "I don't want to hurt her feelings. And I might get in trouble. Can't I do something else?"

"'Fraid not," Colleen answered. "That's what we decided. Don't worry. Come on, Tess. Andrea Blackstone is dying to be a member, and Lauren wants her to join next. But I want you."

"Andrea!" Tess said. "She doesn't even like to hang out with girls. She would rather play touch football with the guys."

"Well," Colleen said, "she wants in."

A minute later Tess agreed. "Okay, I guess I'll do it. Friday?"

"Right!" Colleen texted lots of smiley faces back. "I knew I could count on you. It's going to be great to have you in the club. I've missed you, Tess. Friday night we're having a party—with boys—at Lauren's house. Then the next week we're having a major mall crawl. It'll be great. See you next Friday!"

"Should I text you before then?" Tess asked.

"Um, I think it would be better if we wait until after the initiation. You know how it goes. Okay?"

"Okay," Tess said weakly. "See you. Bye."

This was worse than she had expected. Walking to her mirror, she pulled it close to her face and stared at her eyebrows. "I don't even know Marcia," she said, wrinkling her forehead. "And I never noticed her eyebrows." Something besides the initiation bugged Tess, nagged at the back of her brain. What was it? Something about Colleen and

Marcia and herself, but she couldn't figure out exactly what.

Stepping away from the mirror, she plopped down on the floor. "Oh, well, it'll be okay," she reassured herself. "I deserve to be in the popular group. Marcia isn't even my friend."

Tess stood up, smiling, remembering that Colleen had said she missed Tess. Tess missed Colleen, too. It would be good to be together again. A light rap sounded on her door.

"Can I come in?" Tess's mother stepped into her room.

Tess noticed again how pretty her mom was. Her eyes were the color of summer ivy, and her face was peach-smooth like Tess's. Except her mom had tiny lines here and there, etched through thirty-six years of smiling. Tess was proud of her mom but a little embarrassed when she remembered what Colleen's mom had said about her driving. "Come on in," Tess said.

"I thought you could use some help cleaning your room." Her mom bent over a pile of newly folded clothes and picked them up. After walking to the dresser, she opened one of the drawers and placed the clothes inside.

"Thanks, Mom," Tess said with relief. "I can use the help. It's a mess again." She walked over to her desk and began to sort through papers.

"Are you okay? You look pale." Mom headed toward the closet and sat down on the floor to straighten out Tess's shoes.

"Yeah, I'm okay," she answered, tossing math scratch papers into the trash can.

"I was almost finished but Colleen texted."

"How's she doing? Is she enjoying Mr. Basil's class?"

"I think so," Tess answered. "We haven't talked much this past week." She brightened. "We should be spending more time together soon, though. Colleen started a club and asked me to join. It's called the Coronado Club."

"That's nice. Maybe you can have a club meeting here someday." Finished with the shoes, she moved to the bedside table stereo to stack Tess's books.

"Good idea," said Tess. "Thanks."

"I think we're just about finished in here. Why don't you take a shower now so you don't have to get up early?" Mom put her hands on her hips and surveyed the room. "This room looks great, Tess. I didn't think I would like the pattern you chose, but now I think you were right. The curtains and spread are cheery and positive, like my girl. Better get into the shower." She ruffled Tess's hair before leaving the room.

Tess ambled toward her closet to get her robe. Maybe she should have mentioned the initiation. But she knew her mom wouldn't approve, and Tess didn't want to disappoint her. Of course, she didn't want to disappoint Colleen either.

Sandra Byrd

Chapter Seven
Party Invitation

Tuesday, September 10

Monday cruised by, and soon Tuesday was half over. Although Tess was busy reading at her desk, she knew Ms. Martinez had come back into the room because a gentle scent floated lightly through the air. Tess wondered what kind of perfume Ms. M. wore. It smelled like the lilac bush in Grandma Kate's backyard. Closing her novel, Tess waited for afternoon class to start.

"Okay, sixth graders, please take out your social studies books and open to Chapter Two. Brian, would you read the first section aloud?"

Brian Goldstein stumbled through the passage while Tess watched her teacher. Ms. Martinez's shiny, almost-black hair tumbled down like a molasses waterfall. She wore it pulled back with a large silver-and-turquoise clip. Yesterday, when they had studied immigration, Ms. Martinez had told the class her parents had come to the United States from Mexico twenty-five years ago. They had worked for twenty years doing odd jobs and growing chili peppers in New Mexico until they could afford to buy their own little farm. Ms. Martinez had won a scholarship to Arizona State University; that's how she had become a teacher. She had promised them they would have a Mexico party some day this year.

Brian had finished, and Selinda read now. "Uh-hmm." Tess heard Erin clear her throat and looked over as Erin dropped a note on the floor.

"I know this is sort of late, but do you want to come to my birthday party on Saturday? Circle one: Yes, No Maybe"

Tess chewed on the end of her pen, thinking for a minute before circling "Yes." It probably wouldn't be as much fun as Colleen's sleepover party last summer, but it might be fun to ride horses. Since it wouldn't interfere with Lauren's party on Friday night, why not? Tess wrote to the side of the check mark, "If my mom lets me. Where do you live?" She slid the note across the aisle.

Erin pulled a new piece of paper from her notebook and wrote, "I live in Paradise Valley, but my party is at my grandparents' in Gilbert. I'll give you the invitation at lunch."

"Okay," wrote Tess.

"Well, Tess, are you going to read this section or just what's passed across the aisle?" Ms. Martinez interrupted. She stared at the note until Erin slipped it into her pocket.

"Uh, yes. Sure," Tess answered. "I mean, where are we?"

"Section three."

Tess cleared her throat. "By now the wagon trains had reached the Oregon Territory...." After Tess finished reading the section, the class put away its books and herded to the front of the room to work with maps and computers.

"That was a close one!" Tess breathed to Erin.

"I know. We were almost caught!" Erin replied. "I have an idea. Let's sign our notes with our lip gloss names so if they are intercepted no one will know which of us wrote what."

"Good idea, Mango," said Passion Fruit. "We could seal the notes with a smudge of lip gloss, too. Just for extra protection."

Erin giggled. "I'm glad you're coming to my party."

"A computer opened up," Tess said, glancing at the computer corner. "I think I'll go over there and work for a while."

"Okay," Erin headed back toward her desk.

A minute later Ms. Martinez came up behind Tess, tapping lightly on her screen. "What are you working on?" she asked with a smile, as if to let Tess know all was forgiven regarding the note.

"My geography project. After you talked to us yesterday, I decided to pick Mexico for my country report. It sounded so romantic." Tess blushed, but Ms. M. beamed.

"Well, let me know if I can loan you any books," she said, turning to talk with a student at the next computer. A gentle current of scented air trailed after her as she turned. Silver balls hooped with thin rings swung from her earlobes, tucking into her hair like tiny Saturns deep in a night sky. Once again Tess thought how sophisticated dangling earrings were. She couldn't wait to wear some. She would buy some like Ms. M.'s.

The lunch bell clanged loudly, and the class walked down the hall to the lunchroom. Tess stood in line behind Erin and Jessica. Tater tots, her favorite, were being served. Tess squirted some ketchup onto her tray as the smell of the crispy potatoes mingled with that of her steamy plump hot dog. She plopped into the first open chair, and Erin sat next to her, handing her an invitation with directions to Erin's grandparents' house.

"Who else is coming?"

"Not very many people," admitted Erin. "My mom, my brothers, my cousins, and Jessica, of course. My dad will try to make it, if he's not working. He's a chef and has to work a lot."

"It sounds fun. Are we going to ride your horses?"

"Of course," Erin said. "That's why I'm having it in Gilbert. You can ride Solomon. He'll go easy on you."

Tess smiled; Erin was okay. When Tess glanced over at the Coronado Club table, she saw Colleen, Lauren, and Melody with their heads together. Whispering secrets, she supposed. Tess comforted herself that she would be sitting with them next week. Maybe once she was in the club, she would ask Erin and Jessica to join, too.

A few minutes after Tess finished her after-school snack, she heard, "If I may say so, old girl, you are looking splendiferous today!" Tyler rambled into the room, clutching Hercules' cage while Tess tried on the new hiking shoes Dad had bought her.

"Yeah, and what do you want, Inspector?" Tess responded, knowing his compliments didn't come easily.

"The good lady, our mother, said you would be pleased to let me finish my computer game."

"Well, I'm not pleased about it, but if the good lady, our mother, said so, I suppose I'll let you." Tess tapped on Hercules' cage. "What's up, lizard lips?" Hercules sulked in the cage's corner, innately knowing friend and foe.

"Why didn't you get a dog or something?" Tess asked. "Say, speaking of dogs, where's Big Al today? Does he talk British, too?"

"No, he burps British!" Tyler burst out laughing, back to good old American English again. "Why don't you like Big Al? He's all right once you get to know him."

"No, thanks," Tess said. "I have better taste in friends."

Tyler looked at her for a long moment, then turned to the computer. Tess knew what he was thinking. Where were Tess's friends? Big Al might be rude, but he was loyal to Tyler no matter what. Everyone in the family had figured out that the friendship between Colleen and Tess had cooled; she used to talk about her every night. Yesterday her mom had said, "Well, you know, Lauren was Colleen's friend for years before you met her," as if to give Tess an excuse. She didn't want an excuse. She wanted a friend.

"No, Mom, you just don't get it." Tess had stormed out of the room. Inside, though, she was afraid that her mom did get it. Maybe Tess had been a convenient friend while Lauren was gone but now...

Tess willed the thought out of her mind. Friday was only two days away.

 Chapter Eight
Dear God

Thursday, September 12

Thursday was unusually hot, and after school Tess hung out by the pool, cooling off and listening to music.

Her mom opened the kitchen window and called, "I could use a little help. Would you please come in and put away these groceries?"

"Sure," Tess answered, raising herself from the pool and dripping onto the adjoining patio. The cool water sparkled and shimmered as it slapped against the azure tiles. Tess toweled off lightly, but it wasn't really necessary. The heat would have done the job in less than five minutes. Although it seemed like a luxury to people in other parts of the country, having a pool was nearly a necessity to survive scorching Arizona summers. Almost everyone had one.

The old sliding glass door squeaked its protest as Tess pulled it open, entering the family room. She pulled on her shorts and T-shirt before walking into the kitchen. Seven or eight grocery bags lined the countertops.

"Let's see if you bought anything good," Tess said, more to herself than to her mother. "Hey, chocolate chips!"

"For baking, not eating," warned Mrs. Thomas as Tess started to rip open the bag. "We can bake some cookies later tonight, if you want."

"Okay," Tess said. "What's for dinner?"

"Stir-fry. Want to help?"

"Sure, as long as I don't have to chop the veggies."

Tess's mom tossed the bag of long-grain brown rice toward her and motioned toward the rice steamer. "How is school going? You haven't said much this week."

"All right," Tess answered, running a steady stream of water from the tap into the steamer. "Actually, Ms. Martinez is turning out to be okay. She likes science. Oh, yeah, Erin invited me to her birthday party this weekend."

"Who's Erin? You haven't mentioned her before."

"She sits next to me. I met her last week." Tess said. "Her grandparents have horses in Gilbert, and she's having a few people over to ride this Saturday for her birthday. She's pretty nice. Think I can go?"

"I'll call her mom this evening for the details," Mom answered. "Jot her number down by the phone for me."

Tess fished the invitation out of her pocket. "It's on this. I'll set it on the counter. I need to get to my homework before dinner. It's hard to get it done on hiking nights."

"Okay, honey," her mom said. "Thanks for starting the rice."

Tess turned a cartwheel in the long hallway that led to the bedrooms. She shut her door and slipped on her headphones. She worked better with music. Opening up the book *Viva Mexico*, she started to research her report.

After dinner, Tess and her dad headed for Camelback Mountain. She loved to hike Camelback; it was a tough climb, but the view from the top was spectacular. Last summer, after staying in Missouri with her grandparents, the first thing she recognized from the air on the flight home was Camelback. Its rocky humps slumped over the desert like a tired camel that had stopped for a rest in the middle of the city. Tess reached the top seconds before her dad.

"You're doing well, Tess," he said after catching his breath. A moment later he continued, "I have an idea. My company is sponsoring a Grand Canyon Rim-to-Rim hike next May. We start the hike early, about 4:00 A.M., on a Saturday and walk from the South Rim all the way to the North Rim by dinnertime. Mom and Tyler could drive up with us, drop us off, then drive to the North Rim to meet us. It's a long hike and a challenging one, but I think you can do it. What do you say? Friday is the registration. Should I sign us up?"

"Wow, all the way across the Grand Canyon? I'm not sure." Tess saw her father's jaw harden, if only slightly. He was disappointed. After a minute she said, "It sounds hard, Dad, but I think I can do it. We have lots of time to practice." His face relaxed.

"Not practice," he said with a smile, "train! I know you can do anything you put your mind to. I'll sign us up tomorrow." He sat back, taking a long drink of water.

Oh, yeah. Tomorrow was Friday. She had forgotten about Friday...and Marcia. *Dad thinks I can do anything? If only he knew.* The evening breeze chilled the sweat on her face.

"Tess," he said a few minutes later, "this is the third time I've called you. Are you okay?"

"Yeah, I'm okay. Let's start down now," she answered, stuffing her water bottle into her hiking belt and heading toward the trail. Her dad followed close behind.

"Hey, wait for me!"

Tess shuffled down the path, watching the city lights wink knowingly at each other as the daylight dimmed. Somewhere on the purple mountain a bird called to its mate. It sounded like "Cluck, cluck, cluck. So sad. So sad."

Later that night Tess crawled under the covers, pulling them up to her neck. Her bed normally felt cozy, but tonight she twisted and turned, punching her pillow in a vain attempt to get comfortable. A series of brief raps sounded on her door.

"Yes?"

"It's me—Mom."

"Come in," Tess said. A beam of light angled into

the dark room as her mom opened the door. She high-stepped over piles of clothes and books to squeeze by the foot of the bed.

"Want a cookie?" Her mother held out a plate with several fresh samples. "I know you were too tired to bake them, but I thought you might not be too tired to eat one."

The rich vanilla smell invited Tess to take a cookie, and she did. So did her mom. The cookies were warm, the chocolate chips melted. Mrs. Thomas swallowed her last bite and said, "You were sort of quiet tonight. You don't have to do the Rim-to-Rim, you know. Sometimes your father seems to expect a lot of you, but he just wants you to be the best you can be. We thought you might enjoy it, but Dad will have fun if he goes with the guys from work. Should I tell him not to sign you up?"

"No, I really do want to go. That's not it. I'm just..." Tess paused, wishing she could tell her mom about tomorrow. But she couldn't. "...just tired. I'm sure I'll feel better tomorrow."

"Okay, honey." Her mother smoothed the covers. "I talked to Erin's mom tonight. Everything is set for Saturday. They will drive you out, and I'll pick you up."

"Great," Tess said, cheering up a bit. "Thanks, Mom."

"Good night, sweetheart." She kissed Tess's forehead. "See you tomorrow. I love you."

"I love you, too," Tess answered, as her mother softly pulled the door shut behind her. Tess wished she could have shared her worries with her mom, but, well, she couldn't. She had no one at all to share with. She hadn't even wanted to write in her diary tonight. Balling up her pillow with her fists, she rolled on her side, trying to get comfortable.

Why not pray? she thought. She didn't know much about God, but Janelle, her sometime baby-sitter, said she prayed whenever she needed help. At this point, anything was worth a try.

"Dear God," Tess began, whispering under her covers. "I don't know if that's how I'm supposed to start out, but I don't have any other ideas. Can you hear me? Are you real? Janelle thinks you are. Anyway, I'm supposed to trip Marcia tomorrow, and I'm afraid. I might get in trouble. Besides, I don't even know her, and she might get hurt. But Colleen is my very best friend, if Lauren hasn't stolen her away, that is. If you really can see everything, you know that I had no friends last year. Remember? And I don't want to lose Colleen. I'm not sure what to do."

Tess listened for a voice to answer, but none came. Her body relaxed, though, finally finding a comfortable position in bed. Calm settled around her, and she grew drowsy. Two crickets chirped a rhythmic lullaby outside her bedroom window as she slipped into sleep.

 Chapter Nine
Lunchroom Mess

Friday, September 13

Nothing was calm, however, about Friday's lunch. Tess's fists unclenched long enough to grab a lunch tray from the stack. She balanced her tray on the rail and urged it down the line toward the food. A cool piece of metal flexed against her neck. The necklace, she remembered. She recalled the day last July when Colleen had given it to her.

"Here," Colleen had said, "I brought this back from my trip to San Diego. I saw it in an open market. Right away I knew I had to buy it for you." Colleen had placed the gift into Tess's hand. Tess loved the delicate chain with a charm on it that said "Forever Friends." Immediately she had clasped it around her and hadn't taken it off since.

Now, in the lunchroom, the necklace felt more like a choke collar. "Chicken nuggets or spaghetti?" the lunch lady barked.

"Uh, chicken, I guess."

"What kind of sauce? Barbecue, honey, ranch?" the lunch lady continued. Too many choices.

"Oh, I don't care. Ranch." Tess moved down the aisle, placing a shivering cherry Jell-o on her tray.

As one of the first in the lunchroom, she had her pick of tables. She chose one a few tables back and sat at the end as Colleen had instructed. She settled her tray on the table and stared wistfully down the aisle. *Next week*, she psyched herself, *I'll be sitting at the Coronado Club table with all my friends.* She poked at the chicken with her fork but didn't eat any.

"Hi," Erin said as she sat across from Tess. "New table?"

Erin! Why is she sitting here today? Where's Jessica? Doesn't she usually sit with Jessica? Erin had only sat with Tess a couple of other times. Tess scanned the lunchroom, hoping Marcia hadn't come to school today. Her heart sank. There Marcia stood, at the end of the line. Crumb!

"Oh, change of pace, I guess," Tess responded stickily. Her mouth was dry. Then she remembered something. "Do you know today is Friday the thirteenth? Pretty freaky." She glanced at the lunch line. Marcia was coming closer.

Erin had food in her mouth so she didn't answer right away. The smell of the fried chicken made Tess sick to her stomach. She pushed her tray back. When she glanced at the Coronado Club table, she saw that Colleen and the others were already sitting down. Colleen shot Tess a smile, giving her a "thumbs up."

"I don't believe in Friday the thirteenth," Erin

finally answered.

"You don't? Do you believe in any bad luck? Or good luck?"

"No, I don't believe in superstitions. I believe in God." Erin dunked another chicken nugget in her barbecue sauce. "Do you mind if I eat your chicken? If you're not going to, I mean."

"Go ahead," Tess answered. *How does she stay skinny when she eats so much?*

Tess scanned the lunch line. Marcia was heading down the row toward her. It seemed as if no one else was in the lunchroom except Marcia, who looked so helpless...friendless. She teeter-tottered down the aisle, trying to balance her tray in one hand and an open book in the other. Tess forced her foot out into the aisle. Out of the corner of her eye, she saw Erin smile at her as Erin lifted her milk to her mouth. Tess paused for a second, then, almost too late, pulled her foot back in.

Marcia passed, and Tess looked longingly at the Coronado Club table. Lauren flipped her hair and leaned over to the next table where Andrea sat. She whispered something to Andrea, who nodded. Andrea stuck her foot way, way out into the aisle. Marcia was busy reading her book and didn't realize anything was happening until her spaghetti exploded into the air, falling into her hair. The tray crashed to the floor and milk splashed all over Marcia's shirt. Clattering silverware jumped like frogs on the floor.

The lunch monitor hurried over to Marcia to help

her clean up. The lunchroom echoed with laughter as one student after another howled at the crying Marcia. Spaghetti stuck all over the place, including inside her book. No one noticed as Andrea stood, picked up her tray, and moved to the Coronado Club table. No one except Tess, that is. Colleen gave Tess a disapproving glare then turned away. Lauren put her arm around Andrea. Tess couldn't take any more, so she turned back around in her chair.

"That was really mean," Erin said. "Some people just don't have a clue."

Tess sat quietly in her chair. After a minute she answered, "Yeah, you're right." It was mean. As she stood up, her necklace caught on a loop of fabric in her shirt, and an edge of the charm dug into her flesh. "Let's go," Tess said.

Erin stood up, and they walked outside. As they walked by the Coronado Club table, Tess heard Lauren whisper, "You're a bigger chicken than these blobs they serve for lunch." Tess pretended not to hear or to notice that Colleen didn't look at her. *So much for Lauren's party tonight.*

Chapter Ten
Tom

Saturday, September 14

Tess had consoled herself with the thought that she had the party to go to on Saturday and then surprised herself by how much she was enjoying it.

Cupping her hands around her mouth, Erin shouted, "Pull harder on the left rein."

Tess grasped the tough leather strap in her left hand and gave it a good yank. Immediately, Solomon turned left, and Tess looked back over her shoulder to smile at Erin.

Erin smiled back. She mounted Dustbuster and rode up to Tess's side. "You're doing great for someone who has only ridden a few times. You seem really natural."

"Thanks," Tess said. "Even though I haven't been around horses much, I like them a lot." She patted Solomon's silky coat. It felt like the tassels on top of fresh-picked corn. The beautiful horse had white socks about an eighth of the way up each leg while the rest of his coat was the color of milk chocolate. Tess urged him to go faster, and his feet trampled the reddish desert soil while the wind tossed tumbleweeds around as if they were beach balls.

For at least an hour the girls circled around the corral, finally venturing out into the open acres around the property.

"Are you sure I'm ready for this?" Tess asked her friend, a little nervous at riding into the open.

"Sure I am. I wouldn't let you go if I didn't think so. I've known Solomon practically my whole life, and he'll take care of you."

The horses gentled to a walk, and Erin pulled Dustbuster up alongside Tess. "What do you think of the place?"

"I love it. Do you come here often?"

"Yeah, almost every weekend. It depends on what else is going on. Now that my brother's basketball season has started, we'll probably come by less."

"I'd like to come with you some other time...," Tess said. Her voice trailed off as she became a little embarrassed at inviting herself over.

Erin smiled her big, genuine smile. "That would be great. Jessica is a little afraid of horses, so I don't have many friends to ride with. Hmm." Her smile faded a bit. "Look over there."

"Looks like a monsoon is coming," Tess said after glancing at the sky. Fat black clouds grumbled in the distance, eating up the blue sky as they traveled closer and closer.

"We'd better finish before it starts to rain. Ready to settle for a short ride?" Erin led the way back toward the corral. Tess followed, enjoying the quiet. Slowing Dustbuster to a walk, Erin indicated for Tess to do the same with her mount. The horses sauntered back to the house, where Erin's mom had been keeping a close eye on the girls.

"I'm really sorry Jessica couldn't come," Tess said. She felt bad Erin had only one girl at her party. Not even her best friend could come.

"That's okay," Erin said sadly. "Actually, Jessica might move to Seattle. Her parents are getting a divorce, and Jessica and her mom might have to live with her grandparents until her mom finds a job."

"Wow. That's too bad," Tess said.

"Nothing's for sure yet. Maybe her mom will find a job here," Erin said in a hopeful voice. "She's been my best friend forever and I am praying that she stays."

"I wish Lauren would move," Tess muttered to herself.

The girls finished the rest of the ride in silence.

"Hi, girls!" Erin's mom waved at them. "Lunch is ready. Come on in. We're having a hard time keeping Tom away from the pizza."

"Who's Tom?" Tess dismounted and rubbed Solomon's sweaty coat.

"My brother." Erin jumped off her horse, handing the reins of both horses to her Uncle Albert, who took the mounts into the barn to care for them. The girls headed into the house.

Thick beams crisscrossed the living room ceiling. The worn wood floor was polished to a soft glow.

Navajo rugs graced the walls, and large bunches of fragrant dried flowers rested in burnished brass vases throughout the great room. The curtains were drawn from the windows with twisted black cords tipped with silver. It was a ranch right out of romantic westerns.

"Hey, are we eating or what?" a boy's voice called.

"Tom, meet my friend Tess," Erin said. "Tess, this is my brother Tom."

"Hi," Tom said. At least that's what Tess thought he said. She was too busy staring at his dimpled smile, his tousled blond hair, and his strong hands gripping a basketball. He obviously was the cute boy in Erin's pictures.

Tess hadn't really liked boys too much, and she wasn't sure she actually liked this one, but she might. He looked sort of like a guy on TV, not shrimpy and annoying like sixth-grade boys.

"Don't forget me!" came a voice from beyond the couch.

"Oh, yeah. This is Josh, my little brother." Josh sat on the floor watching a movie.

"Hi, Josh."

"Can we eat now? I'm starving," Tom said as he wrestled Josh to the kitchen table in a friendly, big-brother way. That was cool. A lot of guys might treat their little brother like a bug.

"Sure," Erin's dad said. "Josh, turn off the TV. Let's gather around the table." Why were they gathering around the table?

When everyone reached out both hands and took the hand of the person to either side, Tess was confused but did the same. If she had known they were going to hold hands, she might have tried to stand next to Tom!

Instead, she sandwiched between Erin's grandpa and Josh. Everyone closed their eyes except Tess.

"Lord," Erin's dad started.

Oh, they're praying. More comfortable now that she knew what was happening, Tess closed her eyes.

"On this special day, her birthday, we want to thank you for Erin. She's a wonderful daughter, sister, and granddaughter. Bless her life this year. Help her to love and know you more deeply. Thank you for providing this food. In Jesus' name we pray. Amen." Everyone unclasped hands and looked at each other.

"Erin, why don't you and Tess serve yourselves first? Then we'll follow," Erin's mom said.

"If there's anything left," Josh commented. Just like Tyler.

Most of the birthday party time was spent riding, then eating, but the girls had a little time afterward, too. Erin suggested they play Clue, and Josh and Tom joined them. Tess sneaked a peak at Tom, and he smiled back at her. He didn't seem to think he was too mature to play with them, and he was really nice to Erin. After two games, a familiar honk sounded outside. The rain was pouring now, so Tess figured her mom didn't want to get drenched. "I have to go, Erin. My mom's here."

Sandra Byrd

Erin's mother drew back the curtain from the window and waved toward the car. Erin saw Tess to the door. "Thanks for coming and for the CD. It was fun riding together. We'll have to do it more often."

"I had a good time," Tess said, surprised by the truth. "I'd like to come back. Let's talk about it next week at school."

"Okay." Erin opened the door. "See you later."

Tess dashed out to the car, soaked by the time she got in, and sat down.

"It's pouring all over the valley," her mom said. "A couple of roads are flooded out. We'll have to take it slow." The roads often flooded during the Arizona monsoons. "Did you have a good time?"

"Yeah, I did. Erin's horses were great. I rode pretty fast, and I didn't fall or anything. Also, her grandparents' house was very 'old West,' just like in the movies. I'm sort of hungry, though. Her brothers ate most of the pizza before I could get back for seconds. Her mom offered me something else, but I felt kind of funny and said no."

"I'm glad you enjoyed yourself. You'll have to invite Erin over sometime."

"Okay," said Tess. "She's more fun than I thought she would be."

The two rode together in silence.

"Tess..."

"Yeah?"

"I've been giving it some thought, and well, I guess you're old enough to wear dangling earrings if you want to. It's sometimes hard for me to

56

remember you're becoming a young lady and not still my little girl." Her mom kept her eyes on the road, but Tess could see tiny tears.

"Thanks, Mom. It's okay. Don't worry about it. I haven't been the best person in the world to deal with lately," Tess said.

The radio played softly while the windshield wipers swished back and forth across the glass, creating a comfortable sound. They rode the rest of the way home in the quiet togetherness shared by those who don't need to talk.

Sandra Byrd

Chapter Eleven
Unibrow

Sunday, September 15

The next night Tess could hardly believe her phone screen as she picked it up after her shower. A text from Colleen!

Tess hurried to her room from the bathroom. She quickly unwrapped the towel bee-hived on her head and let her wet hair hang down. After combing it out, she pulled on some sweats, grabbed the phone, and texted back.

"How was your weekend?" Colleen had asked.

"Fine," Tess answered. Why was Colleen talking as if nothing had happened? "How about yours?"

"Okay. Lauren's party was pretty fun. I'm sorry you weren't there, though."

"Well, yeah. I didn't know if I was still invited."

"Oh," Colleen said. "Yeah."

Nothing came through for a minute. Then two. The silence was thick enough that Tess heard her heart pounding in her ears. Was this all Colleen was going to say? Tess twirled a strand of her damp hair around her fingers.

"I really didn't think you would trip Unibrow," Colleen finally texted.

"You didn't?" Tess untwirled the strand she had just coiled up.

"No," answered Colleen. "You're too, well, good. I knew you wouldn't want to get in trouble."

"Then why did you ask me to do it?" Tess's hand tightened around the receiver as she pressed send.

"I'm the club president, but Lauren is actually in charge of initiation. Tripping Unibrow was Lauren's idea."

Well, that explained some things. "But you could have told her no, if you're the president," Tess responded.

"Well." Colleen ignored that statement. "I talked it over with the other members Friday night, and we decided you could be in the club anyway."

"Really? With no initiation? Great!" Tess's hand relaxed.

"Well, not exactly no initiation," Colleen answered. "But we agreed to give you another chance. This time the test is something no one will know you did, and there's no way you can get in trouble."

"What is it?" Tess asked warily, her stomach tingling.

"Tomorrow is a teacher's in-service day, and there's no school, right? So Tuesday, get to school a few minutes before first bell. Take a black Magic Marker, and draw a picture of Unibrow on the mirror of the girls' bathroom. You know, with a fat, black worm for eyebrows. Then write 'Marcia is a hairy unibrow' above it." Colleen sent several winky faces. "No one will know you did it."

"Yeah, but Marcia will still see it. Don't you think she feels bad enough after what Andrea did Friday?" Tess was a little upset, although she didn't know why. She didn't even know Marcia.

"Tess, please do this. I really want you to be in the club. Aren't we good friends?" Colleen pleaded, and added several exclamation points to her text.

"I guess so," Tess slowly typed back. Colleen hadn't said "best friends."

"Then come on. The others all had to be initiated, so they won't let you be in the club unless you are, too. I can't change the rule. Lauren was totally mad when I asked. Don't worry about Marcia. We'll make it up to her. Maybe invite her to a party or something. She'll think she's cool. That will make it okay."

Tess could tell Colleen really wanted Tess to join the Coronado Club. And Tess wanted to. Colleen was a lot of fun, and so were the others, except Lauren, who probably didn't want Tess in the club anyway. Maybe Marcia wouldn't even be in school on Tuesday. If she was, maybe they could make it up to her by inviting her to some parties. Tess would make sure they didn't blow it off, that Marcia got invited. Marcia would never have the chance to hang out with the in-crowd otherwise. And then she could invite Erin, in case Jessica moved.

"Okay," Tess texted.

"Great! I'd better go. My mom's calling. See you Tuesday. Bye!" Colleen sent a smiley face and left.

Tess stared at the phone in her hand for a minute before plugging it in. She pushed herself off the floor to open her door, planning to kiss her parents good night.

She stopped halfway down the hall, hearing loud voices. "Well, do you want me to go alone? Tell them my wife is too busy to visit with them?"

"Don't you think they'll understand that your wife works, too?" Her mom's voice trembled with anger. "I have things to do, too, you know, and I carry more than my share of the housework."

"No one said you don't. But I carry more than half of the income, and I could use your support tomorrow night," her dad answered. His voice was not as loud but just as angry.

"Fine. We'll go to Pinnacle Peak. But if I miss my deadline, who's going to explain that?" Mom stomped toward the hall, and Tess scurried into her room before they met.

"Oh, boy," Tess muttered. Her parents hardly ever disagreed, but when they did, it made Tess nervous.

She wondered if this was how Jessica's parents acted before the divorce. What if Tess's parents were going to divorce, too? Tess closed her door and opened her app.

Dear Diary,

I don't have much to say tonight. The good

news is I can still be in the club. The bad news is I have to get Marcia after all. Good night, Diary. I'll write more tomorrow.

She clicked off before slipping into bed. The sheets rustled crisp and cool against her skin. Her mom must have changed them today. Tess's hand reached under the lampshade and flicked off the light. She leaned forward and pressed her chin against her bent knees. As she stared out her window, a star shot across the inky sky. Tess wished on it. "I wish my parents would make up. I wish Marcia wouldn't come to school on Tuesday."

Do wishes come true? she wondered. *How about prayers? Does God really answer prayers? Erin's family seems to think so, and so does Janelle. Janelle pretty much knows everything.*

"God," Tess whispered, "I miss Colleen. I finally have a friend, which I didn't have all last year after the move. Moving wasn't my idea, remember, even though I know Mom and Dad were thinking it would be great. I want to be popular, and I deserve to be popular just as much as Andrea and Melody, even if I don't play touch football or have dimples. I deserve it more than Lauren, for sure. But I don't want to hurt Marcia. The good thing, though, is if I am in the Coronado Club, I can invite Marcia to parties and stuff, sort of make it up to her. Don't you think that will make it worthwhile? Isn't it how things end up that matters?" Tess sat silently, waiting for God to answer. Nothing seemed to happen.

She looked out over the backyard, noticing the

pool lights were on. Tonight, as it did every night, the cleaning tube snaked around and around the inside of the pool cleaning off the day's almost invisible buildup of slime.

"Help me, God, if you are there," Tess prayed toward the sky. "Somehow tell me what to do." She lay back in bed, wandering between awake and asleep.

 Chapter Twelve
Not Even Janelle

Monday, September 16

Tess rested for a minute on the lawn chair after spending her day off in the backyard, edging the small patch of grass and trimming the azaleas. She heard her mother call, "Come on in, Tess. You've been in the sun long enough." Tess unstuck herself from the chair and headed to the pool, slipping into the water once more to cool off before going into the house.

She figured she had better put on some lotion. Her skin, stretched taut and dry from the chlorine, flaked. A big beach towel hugged her waist like a skirt, tucked in at the top and covering her stomach. Once in the kitchen she pulled a cold soda from the fridge and sat down at the table with some chips and salsa. "Where are you guys going tonight?" she mumbled as a piece of chip fell out of her mouth. She plucked it from her bathing suit, putting the chip on the table.

"Pinnacle Peak Patio," her mom answered, "with Dad's out-of-town guests from work."

"I thought you weren't going," Tess said, trying to sound casual.

"Why ever would you think that?" her mom asked, looking surprised.

"I heard you and Dad arguing last night."

"Tess, you shouldn't listen to other people's conversations," she chided.

"Well, then you shouldn't have a fight in the family room. I was coming out to say good night, that's all. It's not as if I was trying to eavesdrop or anything." It was her house, too, after all.

"You're right," said her mom. "But it wasn't a fight. Dad was tired and worried about a big account, and I was tired and worried about a deadline. The stress got the best of us. What you didn't hear were our apologies later and our agreement to work out the situation for the best for both of us."

"Oh," Tess said.

"It's a normal thing for married people to disagree, Tess."

"I thought people who argued got a divorce."

"Honey, there's a lot more to divorce than that. And Dad and I are definitely not getting a divorce."

"Oh. I wish I could come tonight," Tess said, changing the subject. "I love Pinnacle Peak, even if it is kind of touristy." The rustic restaurant, a big ranch, sat on a mountain crest. Most of the tables were picnic planks set outdoors on a "patio" that held several hundred people. Huge open grills charbroiled thick steaks, and billowy mesquite clouds floated into the air.

"Remember when we took Grandma and Grandpa Thomas?" Tess giggled, and her mom joined her.

"Yes, I'll never forget the look on Mother Thomas's face."

The family had taken Tess's grandparents to the restaurant, and everyone but Grandpa dug into the steaks partnered with tender cornbread, smoky cowboy beans, and lots of other fixings saddled alongside. Grandpa waited patiently, tapping his toes to the live country music while his "well done" steak order was grilled. When the waitress showed up with a boot on his plate, Tyler laughed so hard he nearly choked, but Grandma didn't think it was funny. The waitress finally did serve Grandpa his real dinner.

"Remember when Dad brought the Japanese visitors and one wore a tie?" Tess's mom said, and they both laughed louder.

"Yes. Dad warned his visitors this time—no ties allowed!" The restaurant had a special necktie policy. If anyone wore one, the waitress clipped it off and then tied it to the rafters inside. Thousands of cut ties hung there, attesting to a long history of enforced casual wear.

"Dad did make sure Mr. Kawamoto received a new tie." Mrs. Thomas wiped her eyes, moist from laughing so hard, before continuing. "Janelle is coming over. She'll be here in about an hour. I thought it might be fun for you to have her as company." Janelle was sixteen and lived down the street. Tess thought she was absolutely the best. She had gorgeous, strawberry-blonde hair and drove an old two-seater convertible. She never treated Tess like a little kid but talked to her as if she were an equal. In some ways, Tess considered Janelle more of an older sister than a baby-sitter.

"Great," Tess answered. "What's for dinner?"

"Pizza. I know you just had it at Erin's the other day, but I already promised Tyler."

"No problem. I can always eat more pizza."

"Good. I'll leave cash with Janelle. She can order it as soon as we leave." Mom wiped her hands on a dish-towel and left the room. A few minutes later, Tess heard the shower water running, so she figured Mom was getting ready.

Tess grabbed a book, *A Wrinkle in Time*, and walked back out to the patio. After dragging a chair into the shady area, she opened her book to where she had left off. She must have been reading for quite a while, because the next thing she knew her mom and dad were calling good-bye. A few minutes later Janelle came out.

"Hi, Tess, how's it going?" Janelle smiled at Tess.

"Okay, I guess. Where's Tyler?"

"In the house. He's watching TV until the pizza arrives. How's sixth grade? Did you get The Frog?"

"No, I'm happy to say. I have a new teacher, Ms. Martinez. She lets us have a lot of freedom."

"That's cool," Janelle said. "Are your friends in there, too? Like, um, what was her name? Colleen?"

"Well, no. She's in Mr. Basil's class. Along with everyone else."

"Oh," said Janelle, pulling up a chair. "How's that going?"

"Okay, I guess." After a minute Tess asked, "Janelle, were your friends in the popular group when you were in sixth grade?"

"Some were and some weren't," Janelle answered. "Why?"

"Well, when you were in sixth grade, was it important to be popular? Did you have a lot of friends?"

"I had some friends in sixth grade, not a bunch," Janelle said. "I wasn't friends with the really cool girls because they were sort of bossy. It didn't matter to me because my best friend wasn't in that group."

"That's what I'm afraid of," Tess said, more to herself. "My best friend is popular." Then she asked, "Was it important in seventh grade to be popular? Is it important in high school?"

"Well, it's sometimes easier if you are popular, Tess," Janelle answered. "It seems as if more people like and respect you, and you're in on everything. Sometimes it's not easier. Sometimes there is a lot of pressure to do things to stay popular, like dress a certain way or not get good grades. Is that what you mean?"

"Not really," Tess said. Ho-hum, not even Janelle understood.

"Pizza's here," Tyler called from the house.

Janelle stood up. "I'd better go pay. But

remember, Tess, it's important to have friends you can be yourself with. Friends you can be goofy, sad, and honest with. Friends who like you exactly as you are and encourage you to be yourself." Janelle walked toward the house to pay for the pizza. "Let's go eat."

Tess wished she were as confident as Janelle, that she had a sixth-grade friend like her. She sighed. Yet not even Janelle truly understood. Tess unwound the towel from her waist and pulled on an oversized Mickey Mouse T-shirt. She sat outside for a few minutes and let the evening breeze caress her warm skin. The crickets started up again, chirping in their mysterious code.

Better go and get a piece of pizza. She would need all the strength she could get for tomorrow.

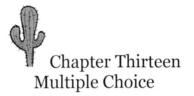

Chapter Thirteen
Multiple Choice

Tuesday, September 17

Tomorrow came soon enough.

"Mom, I have to go to school early today." Tess grabbed her backpack from the kitchen floor. "Can you ask Tyler to walk with Big Al?"

"Sure, Tess. What's up?"

"Oh, nothing." Tess fidgeted, looking at the floor. "I just need to do something early, that's all."

"Okay, honey. Just don't hang around outside the school. Go right in and do your work, okay?"

It'll be work, all right. Tess sat down at the breakfast table, unzipping her backpack. Math book, Mexico report, folder. Rummaging around, she searched for something she had put in there last night, finally finding it. A permanent black marker. She fingered it for a minute before returning it to the pack's bottom and zipping the pack closed.

Morning light glinted off the pretty glass bowl of fruit and yogurt her mom set at Tess's place. Tess picked up her fork to poke at the fruit. Spearing a piece of kiwi, she took a bite, but the fruit stuck first to her tongue and then caught in her throat. "I think I'll just go now." She pushed back her chair and pulled on her backpack as Tyler walked in. "Say, old girl, where are you going so early?" he asked. "Detention?"

"No, I don't have detention," Tess snapped. Her mother stopped wiping the counter and looked at Tess.

"I don't have detention, Mom. Really." Her mom must have believed her because she turned back to the counter.

"See you," Tess called on her way out.

"Bye, honey," her mom said.

"Yeah, 'Bye, honey,'" Tyler mimicked as Tess slammed the door shut.

The day grew comfortably warm as the sun hiked higher and higher up the McDowell Mountains. Tess shuffled down the street, wishing she were already grown up and didn't have to go to school every day. "I'm sick of following rules. I want to make my own choices," she muttered. The neighborhood woke up as the streets hummed with panting joggers and grinding garbage trucks, both consuming excess. Janelle zoomed by in her convertible and beeped at Tess. Tess waved before turning the corner to Coronado Elementary and walking up to the front door.

The sign YOU ARE BECOMING WHO YOU ARE TO BE seemed to shout to her as she entered the school. Walking to the girls' bathroom, Tess pulled open the door. A burst of lemon ammonia assaulted her nose, and she saw the paper-towel holders were stuffed, ready to begin the day. As she stared at the mirror, she figured she had better start to draw before girls came in to check their hair.

Just then she heard footsteps approaching. Tess slipped into a stall so no one would know who was in the bathroom. As she shut herself in the stall, the bathroom door opened.

"She has some unusual ideas for teaching," one voice said. The voice was nasal, sort of whiny. "She's barely out of college and thinks she's going to change the world."

That was Mrs. Lowell. Tess had had Mrs. Lowell for fifth-grade reading.

"'Unusual' is not the word I would use! 'Undisciplined' would be a better choice. Her students will never respect her. I know I don't!" the other voice answered.

Who were they talking about?

"Have you heard about the units she chose for science and technology? And the clothes she wears..." Mrs. Lowell's voice again. "I'd never wear lipstick if my lips were that big. And that turquoise and silver hair clip—she wears it every day! Maybe she should cut off her hair if she can't think of anything else to do with it."

They were talking about Ms. Martinez! A purse clasp snapped, echoing through the bathroom; the door squeaked open, then eased shut. Footsteps grew faint as the two teachers walked farther away. Tess sat still for a minute.

They don't even know Ms. M. The class does so respect her, because she respects them. Her hair clip is pretty, and nobody ever mentioned her lips. Anyway, don't they have anything better to do than to make Ms. M. look bad? Tess knew Ms. Martinez would be hurt if she knew what Mrs. Lowell and the other teacher had been saying.

After another minute Tess decided she had better complete her drawing before anyone else came in. She walked over to the mirror.

After pulling out her marker, Tess zipped up her backpack and hoisted it onto her back so she could make a quick escape. She took a deep breath. Before she could change her mind, she drew a thick, black circle for the face.

Don't you have anything better to do than to make Marcia look bad? she thought. Startled, she realized they were the exact words she had been thinking about Mrs. Lowell. The image of Marcia in the lunchroom on Friday with spaghetti in her hair, crying in front of the whole school, stood out vividly in Tess's mind. Maybe this was the answer Tess had asked for. She stood, eye to eye with her reflection in the mirror, her face framed by the big black circle she had drawn. Then she capped the marker and put it into her pack. Nervously, she straightened her hair in the mirror before going to class. She didn't wait outside Mr. Basil's class today to say hi to Colleen. Tess couldn't face her.

Several hours later the lunch bell rang. Ms. M. signaled to the class to put away their books and papers in preparation for lunch. For the tenth time Tess wondered where Erin was. Of all the days for her not to be here! Now Tess would have to sit alone at lunch. She knew that Colleen and the rest of the Coronado Club would have realized by now that Tess hadn't completed her initiation. She was out of the club forever and for sure this time.

Walking down the hallway to the lunchroom, Tess kept her eyes straight ahead. After piling fries and a cheeseburger on her tray, she sat down. Marcia was in line. She had real guts to show up at school today. Marcia sat next to another girl and started talking to her, and the girl laughed.

Great. Even Marcia had friends, someone to sit with. After finishing her burger, Tess placed her tray on the dish return. She took her paperback outside with her and sat alone. Fifth grade all over again.

Tess had settled into her book, sitting cross-legged on the ground, when a burst of laughter followed by snickering shot across the courtyard, and Tess looked up. Over in the corner were Melody, Andrea, Lauren, and Colleen. They had their heads together but kept glancing at Tess, laughing. Andrea put her hands together so they resembled a book and pretended to read. The other three started to laugh again.

Tess felt her face flush with embarrassment, but she ducked back inside her book, keeping her head down. *Don't cry,* she reminded herself, *don't let them win.* But inside she sobbed for the friend she knew she had lost, and loneliness overcame her.

Sandra Byrd

Chapter Fourteen
True Reflection

Wednesday, September 18

Tess felt somewhat better the next day and was even able to finish all her math problems before the rest of the class. Ho-hum. She chewed her pencil eraser, wishing everyone else would hurry up so they could get on with the next set of problems. Ms. Martinez's pen scratched as she corrected papers. At least if Erin were here Tess could write a note or something. Jessica hadn't come back to school yet, either. Tess wondered if they were somewhere together.

Splat! A spitball stung Tess's arm. She was disgusted to think someone else's spit had touched her skin. Glancing over her shoulder she spied Scott Shearin smirking behind his textbook. Tess felt the immediate need to wash off her arm. She raised her hand, and Ms. M. glanced over the top of her glasses. Her pen stopped scratching on the paper in front of her.

"Miss Thomas? You have a question?"

Tess watched Scott's eyes widen in alarm. Would she tattle?

"Uh, yes. May I go to the rest room?"

"Certainly." Ms. M. handed Tess a pass, then lowered her head to her task again.

Tess smiled as Scott breathed a sigh of relief. She walked toward the door and then down the hallway to the bathroom. The hinges complained loudly as she pulled open the door to the familiar blast of lemon ammonia.

Tess gasped as she faced the mirror. Blood rushed through her neck and into her head, pressing against her eyeballs. The circle she had drawn yesterday had been transformed into a complete face with crossed eyes and a crooked mouth. Worst of all were the huge ears with the word "Dumbo" written in one and "Flyers" in the other. Underneath someone had scrawled, "Mirror, Mirror, on the wall, who's the biggest nerd of all? Tess Thomas!"

Tess turned around and grasped for a stall as acid filled her throat. The ceiling circled the stall as if in orbit, and she couldn't get a deep breath. She rested on the toilet seat. After a few minutes, the acid slunk back into her stomach and the room slowed down, but hot tears still splashed her cheeks. Unlike yesterday, Tess couldn't will herself not to cry. The Coronado Club, of course! But which one drew this? Lauren? Andrea?

Then she remembered. The only person who had heard her called "Dumbo Flyers" last summer was Colleen. Tess couldn't believe it. Not Colleen! Just a few weeks ago, Tess would have defended her friend to anyone, certain Colleen would have done the same for her. And now Colleen had turned on her.

Was Colleen always such a backstabber but Tess had been too blind to see it? Or had Colleen changed? Tess was embarrassed by the thought that other people would see this drawing. Mostly her chest ached at the thought of betrayal by someone who, just this morning, was her best friend. Tess blew her nose on a thin piece of toilet paper and threw it in the toilet before leaving the stall.

She twisted on the water faucet, letting it run as hot as it could while she balled up and soaked several paper towels. After wringing them out, she scrubbed the ugly drawing on the mirror, finally scraping at it in frustration with her fingernails. Nothing happened. It was permanent. Tess slammed the paper towel balls into the garbage and gazed into her reflection.

On one half of the mirror, the ugly drawing stirred up hurt all over again. The other half of the glass revealed her true reflection: red nose, puffy cheeks, big ears. Glancing first at one reflection, then the other, Tess stared at herself, remembering what she had not done yesterday. Marcia could have been standing here instead, crying and feeling sick. Tess imagined Marcia with red nose and puffy cheeks, staring into the mirror at a caricature of herself with a fat unibrow.

Sniffing with satisfaction, Tess was glad she had not made Marcia feel this awful. Nothing could have made up for it, not parties, not fake friends, nothing. Tess recalled the conversation she had overheard between Mrs. Lowell and the other teacher. Maybe Colleen would grow up to be like Mrs. Lowell; Lauren would for sure. Tess snatched a new paper towel out of the dispenser, balled it up, and flung it at the ugly drawing before leaving the bathroom.

As Tess walked into the classroom, Ms. M. motioned for her student to come to her desk. "Are you all right? I was starting to worry."

Grateful that the teacher did not accuse her of slacking off but instead showed concern, Tess decided to talk with her. She probably couldn't hold her hurt in, anyway.

"Can I talk with you outside the room, please?" Tess asked.

Ms. M. took one look at Tess's puffy eyes and agreed. Once out in the hall Tess found it difficult to talk without the tears starting again. "Well, um, there's a picture in the bathroom...on the mirror, I mean," Tess said.

"A picture?"

"Well, a drawing, actually," Tess continued. "Of me. Making fun of me. And it says I'm a nerd." The tears welled up again, brimming over her damp lids. "I tried to wash it off..." She couldn't continue. The tears fell too fast now.

"Don't worry, Tess. I'll ask the janitor to wash it off immediately. That way almost no one will have had a chance to see it."

"You will? Thank you." Tess dabbed her eyes with the tissue Ms. M. pulled from her pocket.

"Can you go back to class?" Ms. M. asked.

"I think so. May I stay in the room for lunch, though?" She did not want to sit in the lunchroom alone today. It might be different if Erin were here.

"I think we can make an exception, due to the circumstances." Tess looked at Ms. M.'s eyes and saw they were soft. Ms. M. really did understand.

"Now, why don't you go back into class, and I'll page the janitor."

Nodding, Tess turned around and gripped the doorknob. Forcing her head up and her eyes straight ahead, she squared her shoulders and strode into the room.

Sandra Byrd

 Chapter Fifteen
Baby Dimples

Wednesday, September 18

It took all Tess's courage to make it through the day.

"Mom, I'm home," she hollered down the hall toward her mother's office as Tess stormed into the house after school. "I'll be in my room."

Before her mom could answer, Tess ran down the hall, tightly shutting her bedroom door. The old wooden trunk her great-grandmother had brought to America squatted in the corner of Tess's room. She sat down cross-legged in front of it.

The leather straps that secured the trunk were almost worn through, and the buckle was banged up from ninety years of use. The lid opened smoothly, though, a testimony to good craftsmanship. The scents of cedar and pine rose as Tess gently lifted out her treasures. Sorting through them, she searched for one particular item. Breathing a sigh of relief, Tess lifted out Baby Dimples.

Fluffy stuffing escaped through a small hole in Baby Dimples' arm, an arm worn through by love. Matted and ratty, Dimples' stiff hair had been styled for years by Tess and her friends. On her tenth birthday, Tess had held a special ceremony for Baby Dimples, explaining that since Tess was too old for dolls now, she would save Baby Dimples for her own daughter to love someday. Afterward, she had wrapped the doll in her soft, fuzzy, pink cotton blanket before placing Baby Dimples inside the wooden chest. Tess rarely brought out the doll, but today she needed Dimples.

With her legs pulled up to her chest, Tess clutched her doll, crying. "God," Tess prayed through her tears, "where are you? If you're really God, why do you let people do mean things that hurt other people? I tried to do the right thing, and look what happened. I'm the one who was hurt. Please, if you're there, God, help me. Answer me, help me feel better." The prayer was barely out of her mouth when Tess heard her mother knock on the door.

"Yes?" Tess called, trying to sound as if she hadn't been crying.

"May I come in?"

"Just a minute." She put Baby Dimples back inside the trunk, closed it, then leaned over to her nightstand for the box of tissues. After blowing her nose and pushing her hair back, Tess called, "Okay, you can come in now."

Her mother sat down on the bed, patting the space next to her with her hand. "Ms. Martinez called me today to tell me what happened."

"Well, don't beat around the bush or anything." Tess sniffed. Her mom reached for a couple of tissues from the box and handed one of them to Tess.

"Do you want to talk about it?"

Getting up from the floor, Tess shook her head no. She sat on the bed next to her mom. "There's nothing much to tell."

"It doesn't sound like nothing to me. From what your teacher said, it sounded pretty serious."

"It was a mean thing done by some rude girls." Tess didn't want to talk about it, but painful feelings forced the words out anyway.

"Do you know who did it?"

"Yes," Tess said, starting to cry again.

"Who?"

"Colleen and Lauren and the Coronado Club," Tess answered between sobs.

"Colleen?" Her mom gasped. "Why on earth would she do such an awful thing?"

One good thing about Tess's mom was that after she asked you a question she waited for you to answer. Even though it took Tess a few minutes, she waited quietly.

"Well, they have this club. And Colleen wanted me to be in it. I wanted to be in it, too. So they said I had to be initiated. Yesterday I was supposed to draw a mean picture of this girl on the bathroom mirror and write something bad under it."

"That's why you wanted to go in early," she said, looking stern.

"Yes, but I couldn't do it." Tess answered.

Her mom tried not to show her relief, but Tess

could see it anyway.

"Well, I guess they thought I was a big chicken, because they were laughing at me during lunch yesterday. Colleen wouldn't even look at me. Then, today I had to go to the bathroom. When I got there, I saw the ugly picture of me on the mirror with crossed eyes and big ears. When I got back to the classroom, Ms. M. said she would have the janitor clean it off right away. Then I guess she called you."

Tess's mother looked as if she were about to cry herself. "How do you know it was Colleen?"

"This summer at swim team one kid told me that my ears were so big they were like Dumbo's Flyers. Colleen was the only one there from school. She knew how much it hurt me to be teased about that."

"Well, I'll tell you what I'm going to do," her mom said. "I'm going right now to call Colleen's mother, Mrs. Clark."

"No, no, no!" Tess waved her arms in the air. "You absolutely can't do that! Everyone will think I'm a baby. It's okay. Really, it is. I can handle it myself, Mom."

Mrs. Thomas seemed doubtful. "All right," she said at last. "But you have to do something. You realize if you don't turn them in, they will probably never be reprimanded for this."

"I know," Tess answered. "I'll take care of it myself."

After a minute her mother said, "Come here. I want to show you something." She took Tess's hands and pulled her up from the bed. "Walk over here."

She led Tess to the full-length swivel mirror. "What do you see?"

Tousled hair. Puffy eyes. Wrinkled shirt. Fat stomach. "A mess," Tess finally answered.

"I don't," said her mom. "I see someone who has the backbone to do what she knows is right. A brave girl, one who had many choices but made the right one, even though it required a big sacrifice. Take pride in knowing that you can still look yourself in the eye. I am proud to call you my daughter." She held back her tears, barely.

Tess squeaked out a grin.

"Now, I bought some frozen yogurt today. Why don't you treat yourself? I need to start dinner. Your dad will be home soon." She opened the door.

"Okay," Tess answered. "Mom, please don't say anything to Dad, all right? I don't really want to talk about this anymore."

Her mom kissed the top of Tess's head. As she turned to leave, something pink and fuzzy in the corner of the room caught her eye. She smiled; it was Baby Dimples' blanket. In Tess's hurry, she had forgotten to wrap the doll back up when she put her away. She turned and winked at Tess, who blushed and smiled back.

Sandra Byrd

Chapter Sixteen
Secret Sisters

Friday, September 20

On Friday Ms. M. began class by saying, "I have something exciting to announce." Just then Erin walked into the classroom, handing Ms. Martinez a pass. Ms. M. nodded, then motioned Erin to her desk. Tess smiled as she sat down.

"I've had a chance to review all the science project suggestions, and I've picked a winner." Everyone leaned forward. "Brad Anderson has proposed building a working model of Mt. Vesuvius and the town of Pompeii. His idea is for us to figure out the dynamics involved in volcanoes and to duplicate them in class. We'll study how the citizens of Pompeii were entombed and learn about the archaeological digs that found the remains of the city. This is an excellent idea," Ms. M. continued, "and I think a winning idea. Congratulations, Brad." Brad's face flushed red, but he smiled.

Tess turned and grinned at him but was secretly disappointed she hadn't won. Science was her strongest subject.

89

At least Joann hadn't won. She was very smart, and she knew it. Her dad was smart, too, and she wanted everyone else to know that. Actually, Joann thought she knew everything. Tess had to admit that Joann did have pretty black hair, which glistened in shiny, beaded cornrows.

"Please choose a partner to work with for the duration of the project, then return to your seats, and open up your math books," Ms. Martinez continued.

Tess leaned across the row to Erin. "Want to be partners for the science project?"

Erin answered. "Sure! But I'm not very smart in science."

"Oh, well, that's okay," said Tess, not knowing what else to say. "Where have you been?"

"I had strep throat, and I couldn't come back to school until today."

"I hope you're feeling better," Tess said.

Ms. Martinez called the class to attention, and they opened their math books. Tess worked on the problems for a few minutes before scribbling to Erin, "My mom is taking me out to lunch tomorrow." Rolling up the note, Tess stuffed it inside a big, fat pen. She passed the pen to Erin, who laughed, then opened it up, plucking out the note.

After reading it, Erin wrote back, "Cool! Your mom sounds great." She passed the note back to Tess.

"Most of the time she is," Tess wrote. "Anyway, she said after lunch I could take a friend with me to the mall if I wanted. Do you want to come?" She put the note back inside the pen and passed it to Erin.

"I'll ask my mom," Erin scribbled, "and call you tonight." She passed it back and went to work on her math, frowning. Erin still had almost half the problems to complete.

At lunch that day Tess sat down across from Erin. Yum, submarine sandwiches and carrot sticks were on the menu. Tess's mouth watered. The sub rolls were soft and fresh, still smelling of yeast and flour. Spicy vinaigrette bathed each half of the roll while colorful layers of Italian cold cuts, cheeses, ripe tomatoes, and crisp lettuce crowded in between.

"Where's Jessica?" Tess asked as Erin bit into her sandwich.

Erin swallowed what was in her mouth before lamenting, "Jessica won't be here anymore. Her mom found a job, and they are moving to Seattle for sure. They'll be back for a few days to pack, but then they're gone."

"I'm sorry," Tess said. "I know you were best friends."

"Yeah, I guess we'll text. I might visit her over Christmas break. Hey, why don't you sit with them anymore?" Erin jerked her thumb toward the Coronado Club table.

"Um, long story," Tess answered, shifting in her seat. She wasn't up to telling Erin about what had happened Wednesday. She would find out about it soon enough.

Erin bit into her cherry cobbler. "You know, the

food here isn't so bad."

"I don't know how you stay skinny when you eat so much."

"That's what my brother Tom says," Erin answered as she took another bite.

"Do you think your brother will be home when I come to pick you up tomorrow?"

"I don't know. Why?" Erin asked, looking at Tess as if she were weird.

"Well," Tess said, "actually, I think he's sort of cute."

"Cute? Oh gross! You have bad taste in boys, Tess. He smells like he's been playing basketball, which he almost always has been."

"I didn't notice," Tess said. "If you want to talk about gross, you should live with my eight-year-old brother, Tyler, for a week. He's obnoxious, and his friend Big Al's great ambition in life is to be in the Belching Hall of Fame."

"Don't forget, I have an eight-year-old brother, too. I'm smooshed right between them. Actually, I've always wanted a sister," Erin confided.

"Me, too," Tess said. "I think it would be so cool to have a sister, maybe even a twin. It would be like having a best friend for life."

"Do you know what would be fun? To pretend we are sisters. You know, Secret Sisters. Like, maybe even at the mall tomorrow, if I can go."

"We don't look anything alike!" Tess said, laughing. But it did sound like a good idea.

"That's okay. Lots of twins don't look alike. They

aren't all identical. Maybe you look like our dad and I look like our mom. It would be fun to pretend at the mall and see how many people we can fool." Erin finished off her sub.

"Okay, let's do it," Tess said. "I could use some fun in my life. Let's go outside." They both stood up and rambled toward the open area.

Tess glanced at Colleen when she passed the Coronado Club table, remembering her promise to her mother to do something about Colleen being so mean. Tess guessed she should talk to her. Maybe after school. No, today her mom was picking them up for Tyler's piano lesson. Monday after school, for sure, when Colleen was alone. Just ask her why she did it, then walk away.

Sandra Byrd

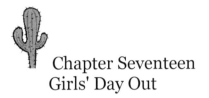

Chapter Seventeen
Girls' Day Out

Saturday, September 21

Before Tess had to face Monday, though, and an encounter with Colleen, Tess savored her fabulous Saturday out with her mother.

"Mom," breathed Tess as she spun around to absorb the restaurant's atmosphere, "this place is absolutely gorgeous!" The ceiling was high, maybe three stories. Huge picture windows framed gardens lush with gnarled orange trees and soft ferns. Buttery yellow linen drapes, richly dotted with wildflowers, were pulled back with ornate brass swags.

"Two for lunch?" The maître d' asked.

"Yes, we have reservations for Thomas," Tess's mom answered.

"Right this way." His crisp black suit rustled slightly as he wove through the dining room, finally arriving at their table. "Here we are, ladies. Your waiter will be with you shortly." As soon as he had seated them and left, a busboy filled their water goblets from a crystal pitcher.

"This is great!" Tess said. "Look at these forks. What do we do with them all?" Silver utensils glistened; their scalloped edges matched the seashell-shaped plates set before them.

"We eat with them!" Mrs. Thomas laughed. "Let's look over the menu."

After long consideration, Tess decided on the chicken salad baked in flaky puff pastry with a salad of oranges, baby lettuce, and toasted almonds. Mom chose a mini filet lightly grilled with garlic butter and caramelized onions. "Let's order Arizona Sunsets to drink," her mom said.

"What are they?" Tess asked excitedly.

"You'll see."

The waiter took their order, and a few minutes later he placed a tall glass on a coaster in front of each of them. The liquid in the bottom of the glasses was ruby red, followed by a bright orange layer, and capped with something fizzy and clear. A long red pick skewered a cherry and an orange slice. "It's cherry syrup, orange juice, and club soda," her mother explained. She reached a long spoon into the glass and stirred. "Try it."

Tess did; it tasted wonderful. "This is a great idea, Mom," she said. "It's fun to go to lunch, you know, just us girls."

"I thought it was important for us to spend some time together. And I wanted to go somewhere special, because of, well, to help make up for the incident at school this week."

"Thanks, Mom. This is really great. And I am

feeling better about the, stuff, you know, at school."

"I'm glad, honey. It's been a tough start, but I just know you're going to have a great year. Look at your new friend, Erin. What a surprise!"

"Yeah, she might turn out to be a very good friend. And I wasn't even expecting her to be!" Tess smiled, twirling a long fork between her fingers.

Her mom smiled back. "Sometimes the very best things are those you can't guess." She twirled her fork, too, as the waiter delivered their food.

After lunch, Mrs. Thomas and Tess drove to pick up Erin. "I thought we might try the new mall," her mother said, "Saguaro Center. They're supposed to have some stores that aren't at Paradise Valley Mall."

"Sounds good to me."

They pulled into Erin's driveway, and both got out so the mothers could meet. After the introductions, Tess said, "Let's go," and the three of them settled in for the drive to the mall. Mrs. Thomas gunned the engine, lurching out of the driveway. The tires squealed like a dog whose tail had just been squashed. Erin looked at Tess and giggled. Tess whispered, "See, what did I tell you?" and both girls giggled again.

Once at the mall, the three of them shopped together for an hour or so before Tess's mom said, "I have a few errands to do by myself. I asked Erin's mom if it was okay if I let you guys go alone for an hour, and she said yes, so long as you don't leave the mall. Why don't you two meet me in the food court in an hour?"

"Yeah!" Tess said. "No problem. Can I have some money?"

"Don't you have any allowance left over?" Her mom frowned.

"Yes, but it's at home. I'll pay you back, I promise."

Mrs. Thomas handed her ten dollars. "Don't forget, one hour. And stay out of trouble." She raised her eyebrows, tilting her head in warning as she left.

"Let's go to Three Squared to check out earrings," Erin said.

"Okay. My mom gave me permission to wear dangly earrings. I want some like Ms. M's."

"Me, too," Erin said.

They walked along, talking about school, movies, and other things until they got to the trendy and cheap jewelry store. Tess scanned the selection, not finding anything.

"What are you looking for?" Erin asked.

"Hey, what about these?" Tess motioned, pointing at a charm bracelet display. "These are great! Do you have one?"

"I used to have one, but I lost it," Erin answered. "You're right. Great chains."

Tess picked out two bracelets, exactly the same. "If we're twins, we should wear matching jewelry."

"I forgot we were going to do that!" Erin laughed. "What a great idea. No one will know the bracelet is our special connection, a secret between sisters."

"Perfect," Tess said. "Let's take them." She paid,

then pocketed the change.

Erin giggled. "Being sisters is fun!"

They window-shopped for a while, and Erin bought a card to send to Jessica. Then they headed toward the food court, but Mrs. Thomas hadn't arrived yet.

"Let's buy a drink." Tess said. "Do you like lemonade?"

"Yeah, I'll order," Erin said as they approached the counter. The teenage girl who waited on them straightened the hat perched on her head, a lemon-yellow beanie with a bright blue propeller.

"Can I help you?" she asked.

"Yes, we'd like two cherry lemonades," Erin said, then turned toward Tess and said, "Twins should do everything alike." Tess giggled.

"Okay, it'll be a minute," the counter girl said. After they paid for their drinks, the girls found a seat in the open area where Mrs. Thomas would be sure to see them.

"It's fun being Secret Sisters," Tess said. "Maybe we could trade clothes sometime."

"Okay," said Erin. "I love your leather vest." She chewed on her lemonade straw. "Hey, I forgot to ask you. Wednesday night at church my youth group leader told us about a huge Harvest Party we're having next month. There will be music, food, games, and a speaker. Do you want to come?"

"Will only people from your church be there, or will other people be there, too?"

"Lots of other people come. It will be fun," Erin

said. "My brother's coming, too," she teased.

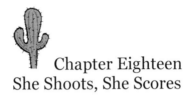 Chapter Eighteen
She Shoots, She Scores

Monday, September 23

This wasn't going to be as easy as Tess had hoped. Beads of sweat coursed down her forehead, stinging her eyes. Monsoon season often brought muggy days like this. Her thick brown hair was matted down, and the books in her pack plastered her T-shirt to her moist skin. As she stood in front of the school, Tyler ran up to her. "Come on, Tess, I want to go home to swim."

"Can you hang out with Big Al for a little while? I'll be ready in a minute. I have to talk with someone, all right?" She gave him an expression that said, "Please give me a break."

"Yeah, okay. But hurry." Tyler lugged his books over to the third-grade hallway, trying to look big. Tess knew Colleen would be waiting in front of the school for her mom to pick her up and take her to ballet as she did every Monday. Sure enough, there was Colleen, leaning against a front wall giggling with Lauren.

Spotting Tess, Lauren turned her back. The

gravel crunched, grinding beneath Tess's feet as she approached Colleen. Adrenaline shot through her blood, making her voice tremble. "Colleen, can I talk with you for a minute? Alone?"

Shrugging her shoulders and tossing her hair, Colleen said, "Sure, why not?" She looked at Lauren. "I'll be right back." Lauren rolled her eyes and stepped aside to let Colleen pass. Colleen and Tess walked a few feet over to a shady spot under a tree. "What do you want?"

"How can you change your feelings toward me so fast?" Tess asked shakily. "Why do you hate me?"

"What makes you think I hate you?" Colleen dug her toe into the ground.

"Because of what you did. Last Wednesday"

"What are you talking about?" Colleen asked innocently.

"Don't act like you don't know," Tess exploded. "You drew that awful picture of me on the bathroom wall and wrote that I was a geek. Some best friend you turned out to be."

"No one ever said we were best friends, Tess," Colleen said coolly. "And if we were, I'm not the one who changed that. You did. Anyway, how do you know I drew the picture?"

"You're the only one who knew about my ears," Tess answered. "And you're the president of the club, so I guess you're in charge. Besides, what do you mean I changed our being best friends?" By now a small crowd was watching the heated exchange from a safe distance.

"Listen. You were a nobody, a nothing. I decided to be friends with you, introduced you to people, shared my friends with you, everything. I really liked you, Tess, because you were different. I only asked you to do one thing," Colleen continued. "And I even gave you a second chance after you wimped out of tripping Unibrow. I had to convince the other club members that you were cool and you would come through. Well, you didn't. You made me look like a fool. You brought this on yourself, Tess Thomas. So don't blame me!" Colleen started to walk back toward Lauren. A bigger crowd had gathered around by now, including Tyler.

"You're a really crummy friend," Tess called as Colleen walked away. "I'm glad I found out now before I told you any more secrets you could blab to the whole school. I'm sorry we ever met."

"Don't think I'm losing any sleep over it," Colleen called back. "You're still a nobody." She linked arms with Lauren.

Tess stood there for a few minutes; people were gawking at her.

"Come on, Tess. Let's go." Tyler pulled on her arm. She scanned the crowd. How embarrassing; everyone was staring. She looked at the ground and headed toward the street with Tyler.

"Watch out!" Tyler jumped to the sidewalk, yanking Tess with him as a car nearly ran them over. Looking up, she was shocked to see Mrs. Clark's minivan pass them and pull to a stop in front of the school.

"Bye," Lauren called as Colleen headed for the car. "I'll call you tonight to plan our next meeting."

Tess could have imagined it, but she thought Lauren was talking loudly to try to make Tess jealous. *Who cares? I don't want to be in your dumb club anyway.*

"Let's go," Tyler insisted, walking toward home. They shuffled along the two blocks home.

Tyler broke the silence. "That was really cool, Tess."

"What was?"

"Standing up to Colleen. She thinks she's the queen of the school. Everyone knows she drew that picture of you on the mirror. She might think you're a nobody, but she's a brat."

"*Third* graders know?" Tess was aghast.

"Yeah, so what? I'm glad you're my sister. Even if you smell." Tyler stuffed his hands in his pockets. "Come on, let's get to the pool."

"Good idea," Tess punched him on the arm, and they ran home.

As they walked up their driveway, zillions of pictures raced through Tess's mind. Colleen. The mirror. Marcia with spaghetti in her hair. Mrs. Lowell's feet. The crowd at the school.

"You're a nobody..." echoed in her mind.

At least this Nobody can look herself in the eye, Tess thought defensively.

She did feel better having confronted Colleen. Fingering her friendship bracelet, she drew comfort from knowing her Secret Sister would stand by her.

Later that evening Tess ate a hearty dinner for a change. Afterward, she helped her mom load the dishwasher, then said, "I'm going to my room for a while. Call me when you guys put in the movie." Her mom loved old movies. Tonight they had rented *Casablanca.*

"Why don't you clean up your room while you're in there?"

Yeah, yeah. Tess opened her door and walked in.

It was pretty messy. Hangers were scattered all over the room like downed electrical wires, and wads of paper, crumpled rejects from last week's homework, lay strewn on the carpet like old popcorn balls. It had been ages since she had cleaned her fishbowl, and Goldy was gasping for air at the top of the slimy green water. She'd clean it tonight for sure. Tess popped in a CD.

"I feel pretty good right now, God," she said aloud. She stopped, surprised to find herself praying. Is that all praying was? Talking? As she picked up some clothes from the floor, something clinked to the ground.

The necklace. Tess bent over and fingered the "Forever Friends" necklace Colleen had given her last summer. Tess had taken it off to go swimming a few days ago and had never put it back on. Too bad Colleen didn't really mean the "forever" part. Tess opened her jewelry box and watched the ballerina dance, swirling in her pink gauze tutu, knowing nothing of the sadness that sometimes came with real people's lives. Lucky dancer. Just as Tess was about to drop the necklace into the box, she changed her mind. "She shoots, she scores!" Tess tossed the necklace, and it banked off the rim of the algae-infested fishbowl before plopping in.

She smiled and clicked on her diary app. After smoothing the gloss on her lips, she wrote,

Dear Diary,

Much too much to write all that has happened, but I promise you it's good. I do miss Colleen, at least the old Colleen, but I'm not sure the old Colleen was ever real. Anyway, we're not best friends now, not even friends really. But I feel okay about that. My feelings aren't hurt so much anymore. Even Tyler was proud of me, for a minute anyway. He'll be back to normal tomorrow, I'm sure.

And I didn't hurt Marcia. I'm not going to be a Mrs. Lowell when I grow up. I do have a friend, after all, and I think she'll be a real friend. One like Janelle said, who likes me just as I am and encourages me to be myself. She's my Secret Sister (I'll explain later). Her name is Erin, and she invited me to a party at her church.

Tess accidentally kicked her big toe into the bottom desk drawer.

Oh yeah, gotta go, Diary. Important business to take care of.

Love, Tess

Tess clicked off and reached into the bottom drawer, pulling out her fifth-grade class picture. She stared at the snapshot of herself, then glanced in the mirror. She seemed different, more mature maybe. Definitely not so sad. Tess set down the picture for a minute. She picked up a paper from her desk, one Ms. Martinez had stuck a smiley-face sticker on and had written "100%! Good Job!" Carefully, so as not to lose the sticky part, Tess peeled the sticker off the paper. She gently laid it onto the class picture, resting the smiley face next to last year's sad face.

This year was definitely *not* fifth grade all over again.

Sandra Byrd

 Have More Fun!!

You and your sis can enjoy an Arizona Sunset together, no matter where you live! Just mix up the following and enjoy!
You'll need:

Two large, clear glasses
One can of 7-Up, Sprite, etc.
One cup of orange juice
Large jar of maraschino cherries
Measuring cups and spoons

Pour 3/4 cup of 7-Up or Sprite into each glass. Wait till it has settled, then add 1/2 cup of orange juice to each. Let settle again.
Grab some measuring spoons, and measure out 2 tablespoons of the cherry liquid from the jar of maraschino cherries. Carefully pour down the inside rim of one glass, then repeat with the next.
Let settle and enjoy!

Sandra Byrd

Secret Sisters

Book Two:
Twenty-One Ponies

Sandra Byrd

Determined to make things right, Tess decides to do one nice thing every day to get back on her mom's good side. Unfortunately, things go from bad to worse when Tess makes another big mistake! How will she ever get her mom to forgive her now?

Two more jobs, and she would have earned forty-five dollars. Surely that would be enough to replace the earrings. Except, they wouldn't be the same ones. She could never really replace the important ones; the ones Grandma Kate had given Mom. Those were gone forever.

Tess sank to her knees and leaned up against her bed. What about praying? Erin's youth pastor said God knew everything about us and saw inside our hearts.

She whispered, "Dear God, please help me replace those earrings. Please help me think before I act. I can't...I can't seem to do anything right. I lost my mom's earrings, and I totally embarrassed myself today in front of my science group with the papier-mâché. When will I do something right? I should probably try to fix this on my own, right? You probably have more important things on your mind, but thanks for listening. Amen."

 Chapter One
Diamond Earrings

Saturday Afternoon, October 12

"Tess, I wish you wouldn't always wait until the last minute to decide what you're going to wear," her mom said. "I don't have time to run around town looking for a costume, and Erin will be here to pick you up right after dinner."

Steam rose from the gurgling iron as Mrs. Thomas set it down to maneuver the shirt she was pressing into a new position. A large wicker basket overflowing with warm, tumbled laundry rested on the family room floor. Beside the basket sat Tess Thomas, drawing a smiley face on the sole of her running shoe with a blue ballpoint pen.

"I didn't! Look." Tess held up a shriveled black cloth. "This was my costume from last year's fifth-grade dress-up day. But when I washed it, it shrank all up, and the fur fell off. Now what?"

"What will everyone else wear?"

"How am I supposed to know? I've never been to a harvest party at a church before. Maybe they'll all dress up as angels!"

"I doubt it," her mom said, smiling. "Why don't you call Erin to see if she has some ideas?"

"All right." Tess lumbered to her feet and started to walk toward her bedroom. What if she stuck out at this party? Would everyone think it was dumb she was there? Would she embarrass herself? She dialed Erin's number.

"Hello?"

"Hi. It's me."

"Hi. Is everything okay? I mean, are you still coming tonight?" Erin sounded concerned.

"Yeah, I just don't know what to wear. Do you have any ideas?" Tess asked.

"Hmm, I don't know. I had a hard time thinking of something myself. Let's see…" Erin's voice trailed off.

Tess twirled a strand of her hair around her finger, then untwirled it before coiling it up a second time. "Why is everyone dressing up? It's not Halloween yet."

"Well, we wanted a chance to wear costumes because we work at the church kiddie carnival on Halloween, and we don't get to have a party ourselves."

"Maybe I shouldn't come," Tess said. "Maybe everyone will think it's weird I'm there. What if you go off with some other friends and leave me standing all alone not knowing anyone?"

"Don't worry! I won't leave you. Besides, I told you other people will be there who aren't from my church. Hey, I have a great idea. Why don't you dress up the same as me? We are Secret Sisters, after all. That way we'll be twins tonight, too, even though no one besides you and me will know our secret."

"Okay," Tess said with relief. She rested her chin in her hand, letting her brown hair rain down around the phone. This was better. If they dressed the same, she would feel more like she belonged. This was Erin's church, after all. "What are you wearing?"

"I'm going to be a snowflake. I'm wearing white jeans, a white T-shirt that I glued silver glitter on in a snowflake pattern, and white sneakers. I guess I'll search through my jewelry to see what would look snowflakey."

"Okay," Tess said. "That's sort of funny. I mean, I don't think it has ever snowed in Scottsdale." In fact, the mid-October Arizona sun generally warmed the days to eighty-five degrees.

"True," Erin said with a giggle.

"I think I can find enough stuff for that costume, Sister!" They both broke out in giggles. "I guess I'll see you about quarter to seven?"

"Yep, we'll be there to pick you up."

"Okay. Bye." Tess clicked off and walked back into the family room.

"Well?" her mother asked.

"She's going to be a snowflake. We thought it would be cool, since we're Secret Sisters, if we dressed alike."

"What's a Secret Sister?"

117

"Well, since we both only have brothers, and since we both wish we had a sister, we decided to be Secret Sisters. You know, pretend we are sisters, but not tell anyone. Like my bracelet." Tess held up her right arm so Mom could see the charm bracelet around her wrist. "Erin and I decided to wear them as our private sign of sisterhood. That's why we bought two exactly alike. Anyway, could I borrow one of Dad's white T-shirts? I don't have one."

"What else does this costume involve?" Mrs. Thomas frowned.

"It's easy, Mom. I promise! I'm going to draw a snowflake on the T-shirt with glue, then sprinkle glitter on it. I'll wear my white jeans and sneakers, if I can find the other one, and some jewelry. Do you have any snowy jewelry?"

"Let me think. I do have a glass-bead necklace you could borrow."

"Thanks, Mom. I'll get it after I've finished with the other stuff. Do we have glitter?"

"In the craft box," she said. "Here, catch." She tossed one of Mr. Thomas's white T-shirts from the laundry basket. It landed on Tess's head, draping over her hair like an old woman's scarf. "Cute, Tess. Why don't you wear it like that?" she teased.

"Right, Mom. I'll be in the kitchen gluing my shirt." Tess pulled the shirt off her head and gave her mother a peck on the cheek.

Rummaging through the kitchen drawers, she found the glue, twisted open the cap, and tried to squirt some on her finger. It spluttered before spitting out a few drops.

Empty. Great.

Hoping this wasn't an indication of how the whole night was going to go, Tess left the kitchen in search of a fresh bottle.

Later, after scarfing down her dinner, she raced back into her room to put on her costume. She pulled on her jeans and looked at herself in her mirror. Biting her lip, she stared at her midriff. Chubby. She pulled on her dad's big T-shirt to hide her stomach. Better.

What if all these church people were holy? What if they didn't like Tess because her family didn't go to church? Well, Erin didn't seem too goody-two-shoes. Neither did Janelle, the sixteen-year-old down the street who stayed with Tess and her brother, Tyler, sometimes when their parents were out late. And Janelle went to church every week.

Tess shook out her brown hair, wishing for the thousandth time that it were straight and shiny instead of wavy and coarse. She could pull it back...nah. Her ears would stick out.

"Don't forget about the necklace," Mrs. Thomas called from the kitchen. "I'm going to Smitty's for some milk. If I'm not back before you go, have a great time. Dad's in the family room."

"Bye, Mom," Tess called back. She almost had forgotten the necklace. After lacing up her shoes, one of which had been stuffed under her bed, Tess headed for her mother's jewelry box.

"Wow, I'd forgotten Mom had so much great

stuff!" Tess marveled as she pulled out one small drawer after another. She supposed, if she were as old as Mom, she would have collected a lot, too. Finding the glass-bead necklace, Tess clasped it around her neck and stared into the mirror. There. That looked good.

But was it good enough? Tess wanted to make the best impression possible on Erin's friends. She didn't want Erin to be embarrassed or sorry she had brought Tess. What could she wear that would be fantastic? A bracelet maybe?

Tess explored the contents of the other drawers and discovered a small box. "What's in here?" Stroking the soft, midnight velvet, she pried up the lid. The hinges worked noiselessly, and as the box opened, Tess gasped. "Mom's wedding earrings!"

The diamond studs glittered like stars in a moonless sky, capturing stray light and then projecting it into a rainbow burst of radiance. Tess knew that these earrings were her mother's most prized possession after her wedding ring and that Grandma Kate had given them to Tess's mother on her wedding day. Tess also knew her mother was saving them for Tess to wear at her wedding.

"I'll just slip them onto my ears for a minute, to see what they look like." Impulsively, she clasped them on and pulled back her hair, just a teeny bit, before glancing into the mirror. The earrings winked at her, gleaming against Tess's chestnut hair. They were beautiful and sophisticated and made Tess feel that way, too.

"What if I borrowed them? They will be mine, after all, and Mom isn't home to ask. I can slip them right back in the box later tonight." Tess stared at her reflection, liking what she saw. She unclasped them and slipped them into her jeans pocket, planning to sneak them on in the car. As she closed the velvet box, the lid snapped loudly, like an angry turtle whose eggs had been stolen.

"Don't worry," Tess reassured. "I'll bring them home safe and sound."

Sandra Byrd

Chapter Two
The Heart of the Matter

Saturday Evening, October 12

"Here, I'll squash over so you have more room." Erin moved to the middle of the backseat, smashing her brother against the opposite door to make room for Tess.

"Hey!" Erin's brother Tom said. "Give me a little space, if you don't mind. I guess I'll move way to the back."

"No, you won't. You know the back doesn't have a seat belt," Mrs. Janssen answered. "Hi, Tess." She smiled at Tess in the rearview mirror. "I'm glad you could come tonight."

"Me, too," Tess answered. "Thanks for the ride."

"Joshua, please turn down that radio," Mrs. Janssen said to her eight-year-old son riding beside her. "I know it's your turn to pick the music, but you don't need to blast us all out of the car."

"Okay, Mom. After this song," Josh answered, and his mom nodded her consent.

"Your costume looks almost the same as mine," Erin said, elbowing Tess lightly. "Can you believe what I found?" She motioned to her ears with the back of her hand, jiggling some snowflake earrings.

"Great! They're perfect. Oh, I almost forgot." Tess pulled her hair away from her face and slipped on the glistening earrings.

Erin's jaw dropped. "Are those real?"

"Yep," Tess answered. "They were a wedding gift from my grandma to my mom."

"That's so cool of your mom to let you borrow them! They're gorgeous."

Tess lowered her voice. "Well, she didn't exactly let me borrow them. But she didn't say no, either. She went to Smitty's for milk, and I just borrowed them on my own. I'll put them back tonight. They'll be mine someday, anyway."

Erin crossed one skinny leg over the other, tugging at her blonde French braid before whispering in Tess's ear, "Well, they are pretty. I hope you're right. My mom would be furious."

Tess elbowed her, giggling uncomfortably.

"What's so funny?" Tom asked. His straw-colored hair framed his cornflower-blue eyes. As Tess studied him, she felt certain she had never seen anyone with such cute dimples.

"Nothing," Erin answered as they pulled up to the church. Tess's stomach buzzed as she saw swarms of kids outside the building. They all seemed to know one another.

"Come on, Tess." Erin nudged her out of the car. "Let's go."

"I'll be here at nine-thirty sharp," said Mrs.

Janssen.

"Okay," Tom and Erin replied in unison. Tom saw his friends and walked over to meet them.

Erin pulled Tess inside. "Let's go meet some of my friends."

Large tables draped with pumpkin- and cranberry-colored cloths lined the back wall of the auditorium, while red and gold autumn leaves decorated the rest of the room. On the tables sat half-empty platters of cookies and chips. Large silver bowls held sparkling punch.

Later, after the activities, when everyone sat down for the program, used cups, some half-full, stood at lonely attention here and there on the tables. Tess and Erin perched on chairs near the front as a big, bearded man strummed a guitar on the stage. Everyone sang along—except Tess. "I don't know any of the words," she whispered in Erin's ear.

"That's okay. Just move your mouth and fake it," Erin whispered back. "Look around. No one's watching you anyway."

Tess scanned the room. Erin was right; no one was looking at her. Feeling safer, Tess mouthed some of the words after hearing the chorus sung a few times. The sweet and sour smells of the room— sweat mixed with perfume, vinyl seats, and sweet treats—tickled her nose. She glanced down at the plastic flag in her hand. The group had just finished playing Capture the Glow-in-the-Dark Flag. Tess's team had won, and her teammates had given her the flag since she was a visitor. This night was turning out all right. Some people wore pretty cool costumes. One person was dressed as a bag of M&M's, and someone else was the Lion from Narnia. Tom was an NBA player, of course.

Tess tugged at her ears again, making sure the earrings were still secure. They were; she would feel better when they were back in the box at home. Why had she ever thought wearing them was a good idea?

"Hey, wake up!" Erin bumped Tess with her elbow.

Tess bumped her back and smiled.

The bearded man left the stage, and the lights dimmed. *Another game*? Tess wondered. But then a man walked onto the stage dressed as a skeleton. You could see his bones and organs, which were cut from glow-in-the-dark plastic. The room grew silent as they waited to see what the skeleton would say.

"Catch!" he called. Velcro ripped as he tore off a fake lung and threw it to the crowd. The girls shrieked, trying to avoid the flying lung, but the guys roared and dove for it like fans scrambling for a stray baseball. "Catch!" he called again and threw another lung, then the liver.

The room swelled with laughter as he un-Velcroed his stomach and tossed it to the crowd, then his intestines. The girl next to Erin squealed and shrank back as the large, squishy tube of intestine landed at her feet. She pinched it between thumb and forefinger, tossing it back over her shoulder.

Tess laughed aloud, enjoying herself. This was church? She had to admit, it was fun. The man ripped off his heart and tossed it into the crowd. Tess watched as a familiar hand reached up and plucked it from the air.

Tom.

After several minutes of wild laughter and gut tossing, the skeleton took off his mask, leaving only his body costume. "Okay, guys, settle down," he said.

"Who is that?" Tess asked.

"Our youth pastor, Jack. He's crazy," Erin said proudly.

"What's he doing?"

"I don't know, but we're sure to find out soon."

"Okay, I know this gut throwing is a lot of fun, but I actually have a reason for it all," Jack continued as the crowd calmed down a bit. "Who can guess what the most important part of my costume is?"

"The part that covered your face. Put it back on, please!" someone called out from the crowd. The room was roaring with laughter once again, and Jack had to whistle into the microphone to calm down the crowd.

"Okay, guys, get a hold of yourselves here. I really want an answer," Jack said with a smile. "What part? What part is most important?"

"The heart," a girl called from a couple of rows behind Tess.

"You're right!" Jack answered. "Who has the heart?"

Tess turned to look where she knew Tom sat.

"Bring it up, please, Tom."

Tom looked flustered but walked toward the front. He handed the heart to Jack before hurrying back to his seat. "Giving your heart away again, huh, Tom?" Jack teased from the stage.

Tess wished Tom would give her his heart. The thought sounded so loud in her head that she turned to see if Erin had heard it, but Erin watched Jack. Tess turned to watch him, too.

Jack stuck the big, red heart back onto his costume. "Okay, now you have a good picture of what God sees when he looks at us. He sees us from the inside out. He's not looking at how expensive your clothes are, how many zits you have, whether you are popular, or if you're the smartest kid in your class. He's thinking about your heart. It's right there, up front, like it is on me."

Tess stared at the costume. Yep, the heart was pretty plain and clear.

"If you are kind, honest, caring, and pure, God sees that. But none of us can always be like that. Not even me!" He smiled. "God also sees the sin in our hearts. Doing bad things, anger, jealousy. There's no hiding any of it."

Tess shuddered a bit when Jack said "doing bad things." She guessed she had done something bad to her mother by taking the earrings.

Jack pointed at his costume. "Next time you're out at the store, or at school, or walking down your street, and you see skeleton Halloween decorations, remember that God cares about what is in your heart. He sees you from the inside out and loves you. Okay, you guys, let's have the guts!"

People with the lungs, liver, stomach, and other organs rushed forward and reattached them to Jack. Tess watched, catching Jack's eye. He smiled at her, and she blushed, wondering if he could possibly have guessed about the "borrowed" earrings.

As he turned away, she stood up. "We had better go, Erin. Your mom will be waiting."

"Yeah, you're right," Erin answered.

They walked toward the door and stepped out into the cool autumn evening. A breeze caressed Tess's cheek, lifting her heavy hair slightly and blowing a cool breath on her sweaty neck. She stood by the curb and unclasped her mother's diamonds, slipping them into her T-shirt pocket right before Erin's mother pulled up. Erin jumped in and scooted over so Tess would fit in the middle. Tess slid over, making room for Tom. A happy ending to a nice night.

"Did you enjoy yourselves?" Erin's mother asked.

"Yeah, it was great. Jack threw his guts at us," Tom said enthusiastically.

"What?" Erin's mom glanced back at them in the rearview mirror as she took off.

"It's a long story, Mom," Erin answered. She settled back into her seat. "Did you have a good time?" she whispered to Tess.

"Yeah, I really did." Tess whispered back, smiling.

129

"Do you want to come with me to church tomorrow?"

"No, I'm hiking with my dad." Tess started to feel cramped in the backseat, hot and uncomfortable. "He couldn't go last Thursday night so we're going tomorrow. Thanks anyway."

"Okay," Erin said. They talked about everything that had happened that night, especially what costumes people wore, until they pulled up to Tess's front door.

Chapter Three
Something Terrible

Saturday Night, October 12

"Hi, guys. I'm home," Tess called down the hall as she slammed the front door on the night behind her.

"We're in the family room, honey," her mom called back. "Come on down and tell us about the party."

Tess's eyes shone, and her cheeks were pink with excitement. "I had a great time. Look!" She proudly held up the plastic flag. "We played Capture the Glow-in-the-Dark Flag, which was totally fun. And they gave me the flag since I was visiting!" She kicked off her sneakers and sat down next to her dad.

"Did you know anyone besides Erin?" her dad asked.

"No, but it was okay. I met the people on my flag team, and we did a lot of stuff in groups. So I didn't feel weird or anything. This guy dressed up like a skeleton and talked about God seeing our hearts. It gave me a lot to think about. I might like to go back sometime." Tess caught a look her dad gave her mother. "Is that okay?"

"We'll see. You had better get to bed so you're ready to hike tomorrow morning." Mr. Thomas ruffled her hair as he stood up. "I'm going to drink a glass of water and then head for bed myself."

A minute later Tess heard him open the freezer door and then the ice tinkled as it dropped into his glass.

"I'm glad you had a good time, honey," her mother said. "I went to church a bit when I was a girl, but after my dad died, we gradually stopped going. I don't know why. I never asked my mom. I guess we were busy with other things." Molly Thomas looked out beyond Tess, talking more to herself than to her daughter.

Then she focused on Tess again. "Well, off to bed. I'm going to finish cleaning the kitchen, then I'm hitting the hay, too."

Tess kissed her mom good night and headed down the hall toward her bedroom. Stopping at the door just before hers, she knocked.

"Tyler?" she called softly. There was no answer. She opened the door a crack and saw eight-year-old Tyler asleep, with his head at the foot of the bed, walkie-talkie still in his hand. She tiptoed in and took the walkie-talkie, covered him with the blanket, and patted his mussed brown hair. "You're okay, I guess, even if you can be a pest."

She glanced over at Hercules, Tyler's pet horned toad. Hercules stirred and threw himself against the side of his glass cage. "Gross!" Tess said. "You are repulsive." Sneaking out backward, she shut the door and walked into her own room.

As she flicked on the light, she reached her hand into her shirt pocket. "Better put these back in Mom's box before Dad goes to bed," she said to herself.

Wait a minute. She felt around in her seemingly empty pocket. "Maybe I put them in my pants pocket," she mumbled, a little panicked now. Grasping hold of each jeans pocket, she pulled them inside out, sure now that they were empty, too. Fear crawled over her like a thousand stinging ants. She pulled out her phone and hoped Erin hadn't gone to sleep yet.

"Erin, something terrible!" she texted. "I can't find my mother's earrings."

"Are you sure?"

"Of course I'm sure! Do you think they could have fallen out in your car?"

"Maybe. I'll check. Hold on."

"Please, God," Tess prayed quietly, "I really am sorry I borrowed those earrings without asking. I'm not just saying that, either. I thought that at the party, too. But now I am going to be totally, totally dead if they are lost. And worse yet, my mom will freak out. Please let them be in the car!" A minute later a text lit up her phone screen.

"I'm sorry, Tess, I couldn't find them. I looked everywhere. I'll put up a note at church tomorrow. Whoever finds them can call me."

"I am going to be in so much trouble!" Tess

started to cry softly.

"Maybe you should tell your mom," Erin texted.

"I can't. I have to find them; they mean so much to her." She texted a frowny face.

"I'll pray for you, Tess. I have to go."

"Bye," Tess texted before clicking off the phone. She clicked her diary app.

Dear Diary,

A major disaster! I borrowed my mom's wedding earrings so I would feel really special tonight, instead of dumb. But I lost them! I checked all my pockets, and they aren't there. Erin even checked her car, but they weren't there either. I know I was wrong, like Jack said, to take them, but I didn't think I'd lose them. My mom will be really mad at me. Maybe she won't trust me anymore. My dad will be really disappointed. Maybe he won't want me to hike the Rim-to-Rim with him in May. Remember? That's when we're going to hike across the Grand Canyon together. What should I do, Diary? Why am I asking you? You're just a diary. I guess I am dumb after all. Impulsive, like my mom says.

Love, Tess

Chapter Four
No Peace

Sunday, October 13

"You're lagging today. What's the matter?" Mr. Thomas waited as Tess came around the bend and caught up with him. A painfully blue Arizona sky glared down on them, the kind of sky that provided no wisp of cloud to cast a shadow, no relief from the brightness.

"I, I don't feel good. Could we sit down for a minute?" Tess hobbled over to a flat patch on the side of the path to sit down. Pulling her knees close to her stomach, she clasped her arms around her legs and said, "I have a stomachache."

"Let's rest for a minute," Dad said. "Maybe you'll feel better after you catch your breath. Are you winded?"

"No, I don't think so."

"Well, we can't let up on training if we still want to hike the Rim-to-Rim together in May. Hiking across the Grand Canyon takes stamina, and you're going to have to build it up." Dad stared at Tess's face, and his tone of voice changed. "Your face looks chalky. No one does her best when she's sick. Do you want to go home?"

"I'm not sure. Can we sit here for a minute?" Resting her chin on her knees, Tess glanced around her. A cholla cactus sprang its spindly sticks out of a lump of brown earth, jumping from the bare landscape like the hair sprouting from an old man's mole. No matter how hard she tried, Tess couldn't forget about the diamond earrings or stop worrying about how she would get them back. She knew her dad was counting on her to finish the hike, but her head throbbed and her stomach flip-flopped inside. "I think we should go, Dad. Maybe I'll feel better when we hike Thursday night."

"Okay. Let's walk down." Tess's father put his arm around her, guiding her slowly down the mountain. "Is everything else all right? Did anyone make fun of you last night at that church?"

"No, I had a great time," Tess said. "It's just, well, I don't know..." Her voice trailed off.

"It's okay. Tell you what: I have to shower because I have a meeting this morning. We can run home, and while I wash up, you and Mom can buy a Sunday paper and bagels. Tyler can make the juice. Maybe a good brunch will quiet your stomach?"

"Okay, Dad." Tess loved bagels. Maybe that would help her think of a plan. She was sure something would come to her.

Later, the tires squealed as her mother gunned the engine and they pulled out of the driveway. For the thousandth time, Tess wondered how such a mild-mannered person could be such a crazy driver. Glad that she still had on her baseball cap from hiking, Tess pulled the bill down lower over her face to hide her embarrassment.

"Are you sure you're feeling okay? Dad said you couldn't finish the hike. Let me see your face."

Tess pulled the cap back up so her mom could look at her. "I'm fine, Mom, really," she insisted. "It's just a stomachache."

"You've had a lot of stomachaches this year. And your color is not good. Could you have eaten anything bad last night?"

"No, I don't think so." Uncomfortable about keeping the secret of the lost earrings from her mother, Tess changed the subject. "I love bagels. This is a great treat. Can we have flavored cream cheese? Can I order a blueberry bagel?"

"Sure. Tyler wants cinnamon-raisin; Dad wants two with garlic. I'm not sure what flavor I want yet. I'll see what looks good when we get there."

A few minutes later Mom jerked the car into Bernie's parking lot. Holding the shop door open for her mother, Tess glanced at the cut-outs of New York skyscrapers that papered the deli's walls. A large stack of the *New York Times* newspaper lay on the counter, dwarfing the small pile of *Arizona Republics*, the local paper. The room was foggy with the warm mist of freshly baked goods while huge wire baskets held stacks of fresh bagels. There must have been thirty kinds to choose from. Exotic fish, such as smoked whitefish, shone from behind a polished glass case, their dead eyes staring blankly at Tess, as if she could help them.

Trying as hard as she could not to glance at the meats, Tess wandered down to pick up one of the *Arizona Republics*. Curiosity won. She glanced in the deli case to see if Bernie, the deli's owner, was still selling the disgusting thing. He was. A large, pickled cow's tongue, looking like a human's but five times bigger, with giant taste buds, seemed to be licking toward the sky. It still had green clover stains on the surface, so it must have been a new one. Tess had refused to believe people sliced cow's tongue to put it in a sandwich, but Bernie said they did. Gross.

After Mrs. Thomas paid for the bagels, they walked back to the car. Mom revved the engine, and they were off. Just as they rounded the corner to their housing development, a car ahead of them slammed on its brakes. A dog had run into the street. Mrs. Thomas quickly applied her brakes, but because she had been following too closely, they came within inches of slamming into the first vehicle. Tess's head was thrown forward, and she found herself staring at the bumper sticker on the car ahead of her. It read, "Know Jesus, Know Peace. No Jesus, No Peace."

"Are you okay?" her mom asked in a shaken voice.

"Yes, I'm okay." Tess said. They took off again and were soon home.

Tess hardly noticed. She was still thinking about the bumper sticker.

Munching her bagel as she read the comics, Tess didn't hear Tyler until he called loudly, "Hey! Are you listening? Check this out!" His eyes lit up as he passed a part of the paper to Tess. She read the ad announcing that the circus was coming to town.

Tess figured there would be no circus for her after her mom and dad found out about the earrings. As she stared at the paper, her eyes lost focus. She imagined it read, "Introducing our new flying trapeze artist, Tess Thomas, age almost twelve, who had to run away and join the circus after being banished for losing family jewels." Snapping back into reality, Tess blinked and figured she had better stay focused. Her family wouldn't send her away.

"Great, Ty. Why don't you ask Mom if you can go?" she said, handing the paper back.

"I already entered Robinsons' contest to win tickets. I'm sure I'll win!" Tyler raced into the kitchen to show the ad to his mom. Maybe if he won four tickets they would let her go anyway.

She stuffed the last piece of bagel into her mouth and sifted through the paper, searching for an article to clip out for her current events assignment. A headline caught her attention, "Police crack down on child labor ring, preteens caught in sweatshop." Well, at least they were earning money.

Hey, maybe that was an idea. She could find a job and buy her mom a new pair of earrings. Tess had no idea how much they cost, but she was sure it couldn't be too much. It seemed like a good idea, but she didn't feel any less anxious. No peace. Oh well, maybe she would be okay once she purchased the new pair. Even better, maybe someone had found them at Erin's church today. She cut out the article and folded the paper before going to call Erin.

Chapter Five
Get a Job

Monday, October 14

"Hi," Tess greeted Erin as soon as Erin walked into the classroom. "I tried to text you all day and night yesterday but you never answered! Is everything okay?"

"Yeah," Erin said. "I lost my phone for a while but I found it behind the dog's crate. How was the rest of your weekend?" She looked at Tess hopefully.

"Terrible, of course. Unless you're going to tell me someone turned in the earrings yesterday at your church."

"Sorry, they didn't. My mom left a note in the church office; so if anyone finds them, that person can call us." Then Erin said cheerfully, "A lot of people asked if you were coming back to church with me. A couple of the girls on your Capture-the-Flag team said they liked getting to know you and wondered if you were coming back."

Tess said, "Yeah, I'd like to. I'm not sure when. That is, if I'm not killed when Mom and Dad find out I've lost the earrings! What am I going to do?"

"I wish I could help you. Let's think about it and talk more at lunch." Erin turned to face the front as Ms. Martinez, their sixth-grade teacher, came in. Her perfume lightly scented the classroom as she walked to her desk. Both girls liked Ms. M. She was young and listened to what her students said. Not that you had to be young for that.

"I hope you all had a really great weekend. I did!" Ms. M. said with a smile. Her pen worked back and forth across her notepad as she took attendance before continuing. "We'll get to current events in a minute, but first I want to give you your writing assignment for next week. I want each of you to write a fairy tale, fable, or story. You can write an original one, or you may rewrite one you have heard. It needs to be at least two pages long. The emphasis should be on the creative aspect of writing and storytelling, not on fact-finding and reporting. Each of you will stand to read your story aloud in class next Thursday. You will be graded on how entertaining the story is, how you interpret the story's message, and elocution."

Scott Shearin's hand shot up. "What's elocution?"

"Elocution refers to how well you are able to read the story aloud," Ms. M. said with a smile. "I think it will be an entertaining day. I'll bring popcorn and juice, and we'll listen to the stories all afternoon. Now, please take out your current events articles, and we'll discuss a few of them. Joann, would you please read yours?"

Tess turned to Erin, rolling her eyes. Joann was a know-it-all. Her report was sure to be on the stock market, which, of course, Joann's daddy knew all about. Then Joann would follow the article with a lecture. Tess could never understand why Ms. M. called on Joann at all. She seemed to actually like Joann!

Tess pulled out a pen and ripped a scrap of paper off her article. She wrote, "My article gave me an idea. How about if I find a job and make enough money to buy a new pair of earrings for my mom?"

She rolled the scrap into a skinny cylinder, leaned way over toward Erin's desk, and dropped it in her outstretched palm.

After reading the note, Erin answered, "Where are you going to get all that money? How much do they cost?"

She passed the note back to Tess.

Tess read it and answered, "I don't know. Let's talk about it at lunch."

She passed the note back to Erin just as Joann finished reading.

Once they were seated in the school cafeteria, Erin poured so much hot sauce on her taco it ran out the corners. The crispy corn shell crunched noisily when Erin took a bite. "So how are you planning to earn the money?" she asked.

"Well, a neighbor lady called me last night to see if I can baby-sit Thursday. I'm really excited. And I think it's for three times."

"You baby-sit?" Erin asked.

"Well, I'm just starting. And my mom says only in the afternoon and for older kids."

"Why don't you tell your mom, Tess?" Erin said before taking another bite. The shell shattered so she scooped up the rest with her fork, holding it together with a blob of sour cream.

"I—I can't."

"Your mom seems nice. She'll be mad, but it's better than keeping a secret. I feel sick when I have a secret. Except a good one that doesn't hurt anyone, like being Secret Sisters," Erin said.

"Actually, I was pretty sick on Sunday," Tess admitted. "And I'm still jittery all the time. But I want to try to fix it myself. Will you come to the mall with me? We can look at earrings to see how much they cost."

"Sure. When?"

"How about Friday after school? I'll ask my mom if she'll drive us; then I'll let you know tomorrow."

"What if your mom finds out about the earrings first?" Erin said.

"I don't think she will. She hardly ever wears that pair."

"Okay. Hey, what are you going to do about the writing assignment?" Erin asked.

"Oh, I'll write a story. My mom is a writer, you know," Tess said proudly. "I guess I must have some of her genes!"

"I'll rewrite one," Erin said glumly. "I'm not smart. I couldn't think up a new story."

"Why do you always say you're not smart?" Tess

144

demanded.

"Because I'm not. I hardly ever get called on, and I've never gotten an A."

"I'll help you, if you want," Tess said.

"Sure. Okay." Erin didn't look too sure or too okay. "Let's go outside."

As they left the cafeteria, Erin asked, "What do you think is up with Ms. M?"

"Well," Tess said, "I did notice a ring on her fourth finger…"

"You're kidding! Do you think she got engaged over the weekend?"

"Maybe," Tess answered. "She said she had had a really great weekend."

"Dreamy," Erin said. "Should we ask her?"

"Maybe. Let's see if the time is right," Tess said. Talking about weddings reminded her of the lost earrings. She wanted to think about something else, anything else.

Later that evening Tess was in her room reading when her mom knocked on the door. "Could you please come out to help Tyler set the table for dinner?"

"Sure, Mom," Tess said. They headed back to the kitchen together. "Hey, where's Mrs. Kim's phone number? I guess I'll call her back and tell her I'll babysit Thursday."

Her mom glanced at her with surprise. "Why the sudden change of heart?"

"Oh, I'm saving money for something," Tess answered, hoping her mother wouldn't press her for details.

Mrs. Thomas walked to the small desk in the kitchen and handed Tess a piece of note paper. "Here's the number. Help Tyler first, though," Mom said.

Tess opened the cupboard where the glasses were kept and took out four plastic ones. She set the blue one at her place, but Tyler yelped, "Blimey! I say, my turn for the blue glass."

"No, 'fraid not, Inspector," Tess answered. Tyler spoke with a British accent half the time—when he remembered, that is. He watched and taped the British mystery shows that played on PBS each week.

"Listen, old girl, give it to me!" Tyler grabbed the glass, and the two of them struggled over it.

"Hey! Calm down, you two! It's not like that glass is the most valuable thing in the world," said her mom.

No, the wedding earrings probably are, Tess thought.

Chapter Six
Ready to Explode

Thursday, October 17

"Okay, sixth graders, please pair up with your science partner. Each pair will join with other groups so we have teams of eight people, each working on a particular part of the Mount Vesuvius project. Remember, the winning class gets to go to the planetarium, so let's all pull together to do our best!" Ms. M. signaled for everyone to move to the science tables in a corner of the classroom.

Tess and Erin grouped together with six others. The rest of the class divided up, too. Ms. M. handed out instruction cards for each team. Joann grabbed the card for their group; she always made sure she was the project leader.

"Okay, you guys, our job is to build the actual volcano," Joann announced. "Could someone get the sack of papier-mâché?" All Joann needed was a clipboard, a whistle, and a cap, and she would be the perfect coach.

After she had turned her back, Jim saluted her before going to the cupboard for the papier-mâché.

147

Tess giggled. She thought Joann was bossy, too.

"I'll get the water," Erin volunteered. Grabbing a plastic watering can, she headed for the drinking fountain. As she left the table, she bumped into Scott Shearin. "Oh, sorry," she said, blushing.

"What should I do?" Tess asked their coach.

"Empty the shredded newspaper into the bowl," Joann answered.

Tess struggled to open the bag, but the plastic was thick. "Does anyone have scissors?" she asked. All the team members shook their heads. "Oh, all right," Tess said, as she ripped open the bag with her teeth. She tore a bit too much, and shredded newspaper spewed from the bag and into her mouth, coating her teeth with the dry, earthy scraps.

"Ha-ha, look, Tess can't wait for lunch!" Scott pointed at her.

"Very funny!" Tess said, wiping the newsprint out of her mouth with quick, embarrassed swipes.

Joann delegated the tasks, and soon they were building their volcano. One person placed the lava ingredients into the test tube, another built the mountain base, and Tess mashed together the shredded paper with her hands. It felt like slippery, wet gum but gritty, too, like gum that had been dropped on the beach. Erin came to help her.

"Are you baby-sitting those kids today?" she asked.

"I guess so," Tess answered.

"Yeah, well, at least it's money!"

"They aren't too bad, actually. I hope I'll make

enough to buy my mom new earrings. Or at least get enough for a down payment!" The goop on Tess's fingers started to harden, and she hurried to sculpt the mountain. She left a small hole at the top for the eruption. Looking at the volcano, she thought how it represented her right now—churning on the inside, sick with pressure, ready to explode. "I hope we can find some new earrings tomorrow," she said uneasily.

"Me, too," Erin said. "What time will you be by to pick me up?"

"I don't know. I'll call you after baby-sitting to let you know."

"Okay."

"Come on, you two," Joann barked. "Pay attention; don't you want to win?"

Erin rolled her eyes at Tess before getting back to work.

"Did you ask Ms. M. about her ring?" Erin whispered.

"What ring?" Joann joined the conversation even though she wasn't invited.

Tess glanced at Erin before answering. "We noticed Ms. Martinez had a new ring on her left hand, fourth finger, you know?"

"Oh," Joann said. "So?"

"Well, we think it's sort of romantic and everything,"

Erin said. "I wonder if she's really engaged. And who her fiancé is. Tess, you go ask her. You're brave."

"What's so good about getting married?" Joann muttered. "It's a stupid idea, if you ask me. It never turns out. Let's get back to our project."

Tess looked over at Erin, who raised her eyebrows. They silently returned to their work.

Later that afternoon Tess went over to the Kims' home to baby-sit. "I do appreciate your coming over," Mrs. Kim said. "I'm sure you'll have a fun time with the boys. After all, you have lots of experience with your own brother!" She smiled as she closed the front door, locking Tess in the jail cell with the two boys.

"Okay, guys, what do you want to do, play some games?" Although Tess grumbled, she enjoyed kids, even active ones like Jerry and Joe. As long as they didn't act up.

"No, we want to make a snack," Jerry said.

"Okay," Tess said. "Let's go into the kitchen." They walked from the front hallway into the kitchen.

This was Tess's first baby-sitting job for pay, but she wasn't nervous. She had helped out with Tyler ever since he was born, and she was always in charge of the kids at the family reunion.

"How about a peanut butter and jelly sandwich?" Joe suggested.

"Sure," Tess said. "You guys get the stuff out while I go to the bathroom."

She raced down the hall as quickly as she could, not wanting to leave them alone for too long. A minute or two later, on her way back down the hallway, she heard giggling from the kitchen.

Picking up her pace, she gasped as she entered the room. Blobs of peanut butter covered the beautiful wallpaper of Mrs. Kim's neat kitchen. Joe loaded another blob into his spoon, which he was using as a slingshot, ready to fire another round.

Tess stepped into the room and cried out, "Stop! What are you doing?"

"Nothing," Jerry answered. Then he yelped as Joe nailed him with the blob.

"Okay, you two, cut it out right away, or I'll call your dad at work."

The boys sobered up.

"Now, we have to clean up this mess. Where are the towels?" Tess asked.

Fifteen minutes later, after wiping up the kitchen, she suggested a video, which calmed the boys down, and then a game of checkers in the family room. They played that and several other games for the next couple of hours until Mrs. Kim came home.

"Thanks again, Tess. I'll see you on Monday, same time." She slipped two bills into Tess's hand. Tess stuffed them into her pocket and headed down the street and into her house. She didn't want Mrs. Kim to see her examining the money, even though she was eager to find out how much she had earned.

"Anyone here?" she called into the family room.

"I'm in the office, honey," her mom answered from down the hall. Tess walked into the tiny office next to her parents' bedroom. Mrs. Thomas wrote television and radio commercials and magazine ads

151

for a big advertising agency in Los Angeles, working from her home office.

"How did it go?" she asked.

"Okay, I guess. Tyler is an angel compared to those two! Where is Tyler, anyway?"

"As usual, he is at his pal's house, Big Al. I can't wait for him to come home. He received an envelope in the mail from Robinsons-May. I think it's circus tickets. He must have won their contest. I can't imagine what else he would get from them."

"Great!" Tess said. "He's going to be psyched. Maybe he can take Big Al, too, and leave him there. He would fit right in with the clowns." Big Al was a gross, burping twerp as far as Tess was concerned. She couldn't imagine what Tyler saw in him.

"Tess, be kind. Why don't you get a jump-start on your homework? Oh, and Erin called."

"She must want to know what time we're going to the mall tomorrow," Tess said.

"We can pick her up about three-thirty. I wish you would tell me what you're looking for. Maybe I could make a suggestion."

"Um, no thanks, Mom," Tess said nervously. "I'd better start on my homework." Heading toward her room, she fished the bills out of her pocket. Fifteen dollars!

Two more jobs, and she would have earned forty-five dollars. Surely that would be enough to replace the earrings. Except, they wouldn't be the same ones. She could never really replace the important ones; the ones Grandma Kate had given Mom.

Those were gone forever.

Tess sank to her knees and leaned up against her bed. What about praying? Erin's youth pastor said God knew everything about us and saw inside our hearts.

She whispered, "Dear God, please help me replace those earrings. Please help me think before I act. I can't...I can't seem to do anything right. I lost my mom's earrings, and I totally embarrassed myself today in front of my science group with the papier-mâché. When will I do something right? I should probably try to fix this on my own, right? You probably have more important things on your mind, but thanks for listening. Amen."

 Chapter Seven
Losing Heart

Friday, October 18

"Okay, let's look at the directory and see where the jewelry stores are." Tess eagerly strode to one of the tall, three-sided mall directories. Erin followed, and the two scanned the list.

"Here's one," Erin said. "I think that's where my mom buys her watch batteries. That store must be okay. Let's go!" The two girls hurried through the mall toward the jeweler's.

"How much did you make yesterday?" Erin asked.

"Fifteen dollars. I'm going to watch the boys two more times in the next two weeks so I should make forty-five dollars. Do you think that's enough?"

"I don't know, Tess. Those earrings were awfully nice. I wish someone had found them."

"Me, too," Tess said. "Look, here we are."

The two girls rushed into the jeweler's and looked around. The glass cases shimmered, showcasing precious gems, shiny gold, polished silver, all of which rested on a bed of forest-green

155

velour. "Why is everything always shiny and bright in the jewelry stores, but when you actually see people wearing those things they don't look the same?" Tess asked.

"I wondered that, too, so last time we were in here I asked my mom," Erin said. "Look up."

Tess did. "Wow! Check out those lights." At least a hundred light bulbs were recessed into the store's ceiling, shining majestically on the jewelry below. "Besides," Tess added, "they probably polish the jewelry every day."

"May I help you girls?" An older saleslady with half-moon glasses approached them with a certain air of disapproval.

"Yes," Tess said, "we would like to see some diamond earrings."

"Really?" The lady smiled, but the smile seemed insincere.

Annoyed now, Tess said, "Yes, I'd like to see those right there." She pointed to a pair of diamond studs nestled in the showcase, a pair about the same size as the ones she had lost. The saleslady turned to the security guard, winking before fingering the many keys on her chain. At least twenty-five keys swung from an expandable wrist band. Finding the right key, she inserted it into the small lock and reached in, sliding out the pair Tess had indicated. After briefly looking them over, Tess decided they were almost a perfect match.

"How much are they?"

The saleslady turned over the box. "Five hundred

dollars."

"Five hundred dollars!" Tess shouted, shocked. "Do you have anything cheaper?" The hundred lights were bearing down on her now, pointing her out, like the floodlights of a police lineup.

"Nothing of this size or quality, I'm afraid." After replacing the gems in their velour nest, the saleslady locked up the case again. "May I help you with anything else?"

"No—no, thank you," Tess answered, stunned.

"Come on, Tess, let's get something to drink," Erin said, urging Tess out of the store. They walked a short way to the food court to order a lemonade.

After sitting there for a minute, Tess said, "Well, I'm dead. I might as well kiss my life good-bye. There is no way I can make five hundred dollars, ever. What am I going to do?" Blood rushed into Tess's face, and she blinked fast.

As Tess sniffed, Erin reached across the table to pat her friend's arm. "I wish I could help."

Tess stood up and pulled a dime out of her pocket. After walking a few steps, she threw it into the wishing well stationed in the middle of the food court. Then she came back and sat down.

"What was that all about?" Erin asked.

"I wished that the earrings would come back," Tess said.

"I don't think wishing wells work, silly!" Erin said. "Have you prayed about the earrings?"

"Yes!" Tess said. "As matter of fact, I did the other night. And did anything happen? No. I don't think God answers prayers." Even as she said it, Tess knew it wasn't true, but she was angry.

"God doesn't give us a yes answer every time, Tess. Besides, don't be mad at God. You were the one who took those earrings without asking, not him. Did you only pray once? When you want something really bad, like a new bike, or to go to a movie or something, do you only ask your parents once? No! You keep asking, politely, over and over. Why don't you keep praying?"

"I suppose. I don't think God cares too much about me. I can't do anything right. I'm not special. And now," Tess sniffed, "I'm going to have to tell my mom."

"I know," Erin said. "I'll pray, too. You're my Secret Sister, right? And a sister will never let you down! I'll stick by you no matter what, even if you get in totally big trouble."

Tess reached over to squeeze her friend's hand. "Thanks. I'm glad we're friends."

Erin smiled. "Me, too."

They stood up and headed through the mall toward the front door. As they passed the stores, Tess noticed almost everyone had Halloween decorations. Suddenly she stopped. In one window a cardboard skeleton waved at her. It seemed to stare right at her, with its limbs all askew.

"Remember what Jack said about skeletons?" she asked Erin.

"Yes, I do." Erin seemed surprised Tess remembered.

"Let's go," she said to Erin. "My mom will be here soon. I had better get ready to tell her. I guess I would have to tell her anyway. Even if I could have bought another pair, it wouldn't be the same pair." The two of them walked outside, leaving the skeleton behind.

Sandra Byrd

Chapter Eight
Confession

Friday Afternoon, October 18

"You were awfully quiet the whole way home, Tess." Her mother looked at her. "Are you feeling okay? I think I'd better make an appointment with Dr. Irvine. You've had a lot of stomachaches the past couple of months." Mom slid her keys onto the hook inside the front door and hung her purse over a doorknob.

"Jolly good news, lassie!" Tyler zoomed through the room waving something in the air.

"What do you have?" Tess asked.

"Circus tickets!" Tyler said gleefully.

"I thought the letter from Robinson's said someone else won."

"Yes, but Mom and Dad decided we could go on discount family night, anyway. That's Monday. And I'm even going to let you come!" He slid out of the tiled hallway and into the family room, skating on his socks.

Well, now or never. "Uh, Mom, could I talk with you for a minute?"

"Sure, honey. What is it?"

161

"Well, can we talk in private?" Tess fidgeted, staring down at her scuffed shoe tops.

"Sure. Let's go in your room," she suggested. They walked into Tess's room and sat down on her bed.

"Well, you know how I was really nervous about going to that Harvest Party last weekend?" Tess started.

"Yes..."

"Well, I thought if I wore something nice, something special, I'd feel special, too."

"I thought you looked nice, Tess."

"I wanted to look even better. So, after I got out your glass-bead necklace, I searched around for a bracelet or something else." Mrs. Thomas sat quietly, and Tess gulped before continuing. "I found your velvet earring box. And when I opened it, I saw your wedding earrings. They looked so beautiful that I wanted to try them on. And when I did, I knew they would be perfect, and you weren't home to ask, but I wore them to the party anyway."

"Tess, you didn't! Those are precious to me. They should be to you, too. They'll be yours someday. But for now, they're still mine. I'm disappointed in your decision, sneaking something out of the house and then sneaking it back in. That's stealing!"

Slow tears rolled down Tess's cheeks, and the production line sped up as her mom talked. Tess felt tiny blotches break out all over her cheeks.

"That's the problem, Mom. I didn't sneak them back in. I couldn't. When I got home and reached into my pocket to put them away—" Tess's voice broke as she sobbed out the last few words. "—they were gone!"

"Gone? What do you mean? Lost?" Her mother's face was flushed now, too. Tess knew she was angry.

"I put them in my pocket while I waited for Erin's mother to come and get us. At least, that's what I thought happened. They must have fallen out or something because, when I got home, they were gone. Erin checked in her car, and they weren't there either." She cried louder. "I didn't mean to steal them. I just wanted to look nice."

Mrs. Thomas stood up and paced around the bedroom. "Whatever got into you? Where did you get the idea that you could 'borrow' something of mine without asking? How would you feel if I sneaked into your wooden chest and took Baby Dimples out for one of my friend's daughters to play with? And then she lost her, and you never got her back?" Her mom ripped a tissue out of the box to blow her nose.

"I know it's awful, Mom. I'm so sorry. Please don't hate me." Cupping her hands over her face, Tess cried.

Finally ending her mad waltz around the room, Mrs. Thomas sat down on the bed next to Tess and reached over, pulling Tess closer. "I would never hate you, Tess. I love you. I always will." Tess quieted some. "But I'm sad. Those earrings meant a lot to me. They were a wedding gift from my mother, and I had hoped that you, too, would wear them at your wedding."

"I know, Mom. I'm sorry. I wanted to buy some new ones for you. That's why I went to the mall." Her mother pulled Tess away from her so she could look at Tess's face. Tess wiped her hands under her puffy eyes, splashing aside the last tears. "But they cost five hundred dollars, and I only made fifteen dollars babysitting. I'm sorry."

Tears dripped down her mom's cheeks now, too, which made Tess start crying all over again. "I'm glad you wanted to fix the situation, Tess. But you should have come to me right away. Replacing the earrings without telling me would only have made the matter worse. It would have been lying on top of stealing." Tess's mom twisted her hands together, rubbing her wedding ring. That's what she did whenever she was agitated.

"Maybe someone will find them. Erin's mother put a note on the door at her church. So if anyone sees them, he'll call her."

"Tess, that is not going to happen. It's been a whole week. And those earrings are expensive. If someone found them, he would think it was his lucky day and keep them." She sniffed, and Tess sniffed, too. Finally, she stood up. "I hope you understand the seriousness of what you have done— stealing and lying. Do you realize now how your impulsiveness will lead you to do wrong and how it can hurt others?"

"Yes, I do, Mom. I'll make it up to you, I promise."

"I think your father will want to talk with you, too. I'll call you at dinnertime." Mrs. Thomas sniffed again before pulling the door shut behind her.

An hour later, a puffy-faced, red-nosed, stuffed-up, and cried-out Tess clicked into her diary.

Dear Diary,

Well, I've blown it again. Now Mom knows the awful truth about her earrings, and, just like I told you, she cried. What a dope I am. Why did I take those earrings anyway?

Anyway, I'm going to try very hard to do some special things for my mom around the house, something good every day, like laundry or whatever. I love my mom. I feel so bad I lost her earrings.

Love, Tess

She turned off the phone and pulled out a sheet of paper from her school notebook. She wrote in big letters: "Please do not disturb. Please leave dinner outside of door. I'll see everyone tomorrow. Love, Tess." She grabbed some tape and stuck the note to the outside of her door. There. Now they could enjoy their dinner and Tyler's plans for the circus without her ruining everything.

A few minutes later she pulled off her earphones to hear the increasingly loud knocking at her door. "Who is it?" she called.

"Dad."

Oh great, now she was really in for it. "Come in,"

she said, trying to be brave.

He opened the door, handing her a plate with dinner on it. "Your mother told me what happened. I want you to know how upset I am. Time and time again we have talked about how you must think before you act. This time you didn't, and look at the results." His face was red, and his head shook as he talked in a rough, barely controlled voice, sure signs of extreme anger.

"I know." Tess picked at the peas on her plate.

He sat down next to her. "Remember when you took the binoculars out of the front hall closet to look at birds? It took me a whole year to save up to buy a new pair after you dropped them. And now the earrings, which can't be replaced. Your mother and I love you, but we need to figure out what is going to get this lesson through your head. I am serious. No phone? No parties? What's it going to take?" Dad stroked the bald spot on the top of his head.

"I understand now, Dad. I really do. And I'm going to do special stuff for Mom every day to make it up to her. I promise I will think before I act from now on. I promise."

"We'll see. There will be some other discipline. I'll talk about it with Mom. Now eat your dinner and finish your homework." He squeezed her shoulder as he stood up to leave the room.

Tess watched her fish swim placidly in its algae-infested bowl. "I have to learn to think, Goldy," she said. Goldy stared back at her for a minute, then continued her laps around the bowl.

Chapter Nine
Something Wonderful

Saturday, October 19

Tess could feel the gritty cleanser on her fingernails. Her hands were tight and dry with bleach residue as she scrubbed the bathtub, propping her knees against its cool side. Her legs ached when she finally stood to survey her work. There, that looked good. She had even scraped the fungus from the rubber strips lining the shower. Gleaming glass smiled down on her from the mirror. Not a trace of Tyler's toothpaste spit could be seen in the sink. Satisfied, she rinsed and dried her hands.

Mom would surely love this. She hated cleaning the bathrooms. What a surprise it would be when she discovered this one was done. Tess wished she could be around to see what happened, but she liked the idea of surprising her mom more.

"Tess, are you ready to go?" Mrs. Thomas called out from the family room. "Dad wants to take you to Erin's in fifteen minutes so he can come home to trim the palm trees."

Tess called back, "I'll be ready in a minute." She

flipped off the bathroom light and turned toward her bedroom to change her clothes. She felt better today, being able to make up the loss of the earrings to her mother. And no matter what her mom said, Tess was going to do something wonderful for her every day this week.

Soon Tess was swiveling back and forth on the breakfast stool in Erin's kitchen. "Well, how did she take it?" Erin asked.

"I don't know. Okay, I guess. I thought she would be a lot madder, but sometimes it depends on her mood. I hate it when my mom cries. That's the worst. And, of course, she did. I know she's disappointed. She said I stole the earrings. I didn't think I was stealing them; I thought I was borrowing them...without asking."

"Well, you're obviously not grounded since you're here."

"Yeah, well, something worse. I was supposed to be able to start walking to the store by myself, just to Smitty's and Taco Bell. But Dad said since I wasn't making responsible decisions, I can only go with an adult."

"Oh. Sorry," Erin said. "I like going by myself. It's the only freedom I have some days."

"I know. I was looking forward to it. Oh well, he said he would reevaluate in a few months." Tess looked as if she might cry again. Then she brightened. "But I am making it up to my mom, doing special stuff for her every day this week. Like today I cleaned the bathroom."

"I folded all the laundry last time I sassed my mother," Erin said. "I think she was glad I knew I had done something wrong." Erin pulled some lunch meat and mayonnaise out of the refrigerator. "Do you want cheese on your sandwich?" she asked.

"Okay," Tess answered. "If you have orange cheese. I don't like white cheese."

"Me either. That's so weird, like we really are sisters! Will you grab the bag of chips out of the cupboard behind you?" Erin finished making the sandwiches and put them into a picnic basket. "Do we want a blanket?"

"Yeah, that would be fun."

"Okay," Erin said, "I'll get one." A few seconds later she returned with a ragged purple blanket. "It's sort of old, but at least my mom won't care if it gets a little dirty." The two of them headed out into Erin's backyard. "Was that your dad who dropped you off?"

"Yeah," Tess answered.

"I wish my dad were home on Saturdays," Erin lamented. "He's gone a lot. But he is trying to figure out how he can spend more time at home. He says the restaurant falls apart when he's not there. As the head chef, he doesn't trust the other chefs to do everything like he does."

They spread out their blanket under a gnarled pecan tree. "If we pick up some of the nut shells, this would be a good place to sit," Erin said.

"Did I tell you we're going to the circus Monday?" Tess asked.

"How fun! Your brother won those tickets?"

"No, but my parents knew how much he wanted to go; so they bought tickets for discount family night this Monday. I guess we'll go after I baby-sit."

"Are you still baby-sitting? I mean, now that you can't buy your mom the earrings?" Erin asked.

"Yeah, this coming Monday; also next week, if she needs me. It's really sort of fun. And the money is good."

"I bet. I wish someone would ask me to baby-sit! What are you going to do with the money?"

"I don't know," Tess answered. She took a bite of her sandwich, chewed for a moment, and said, "Remember last Saturday night when Jack talked about sin?"

Erin finished her chip. "Yes."

"Well, I—I'm not sure I know what sin is. Is it stealing? Or killing people? Or what? I don't think I'm really bad even if I do make some mistakes," Tess finished.

"Everybody sins, which is just making wrong choices. Doing something other than what God wants for them, whether they meant to do it or not," Erin said. "I'm not sure where it says that, or the exact words, actually." Her cheeks turned valentine red. "But I can look it up or ask my brother and tell you next week."

"No, don't ask your brother. I'd be sort of embarrassed if he knew I didn't know what it was," Tess said.

"Maybe I can ask my Sunday school teacher,"

Erin offered.

"Okay."

"Do you want to come to church with me tomorrow?"

"No, thanks," Tess said. She peeled her orange and popped a section in her mouth. After swallowing she continued, "I think I'll do the laundry for my mom, then I have to write my fairy tale. Do you know what you're going to write yet?"

"No, I can't think of anything. I want it to be good. And I won't have too much time to write. Tomorrow is church, and tomorrow night we're going back because it's missionary night."

"You go to church on Sunday nights, too? Isn't that a lot? Don't you get sick of it?"

"I do get bored sometimes," Erin said. "But we don't go every Sunday night. And I know I won't be bored this Sunday night because the missionaries tell stories about the cool places they live and about the people they live with. And they show slides."

"Oh," Tess said, "that does sound fun." She wrapped her orange peel in her napkin before plopping it into the basket. "I guess I won't be having fun anymore." Tess picked at her sandwich crust and looked toward the ground.

"Don't worry, Tess. It will turn out all right. I'm sure your mom thinks you're more important than any earrings. And you have me, right? We're sisters. Let's change the subject and think of some fun stuff to do together. I've been thinking about a few things."

"Yeah?" Tess looked up, smiling at last. "Like what?"

"Well," Erin continued, "since we're almost the same size, what if I put together an outfit for you from my clothes, and you put one together for me out of your clothes. We'll meet in the bathroom before first bell."

"Okay, then what?"

"Then we change clothes! We really have to trust the other person not to pick out something dorky for us to wear."

"Cool. Let's do it! How about Tuesday, since we're going to the circus Monday night?"

"Okay," Erin answered. They swapped Secret Sister bracelets to close the deal, which they always did to seal a promise. Tess popped the last bite of sandwich into her mouth, already planning what Erin would wear.

Chapter Ten
Three-Ring Circus

Monday, October 21

"No way," Tess said, hands on hips and mouth pursed. "You guys are not fixing another snack by yourselves. Remember the peanut butter cocoons hanging from the wallpaper last time I was here? I'll help you."

Tess marched the two Kim boys into the kitchen and found a bag of microwave popcorn. While waiting for the popping to stop, she mixed up a can of juice. She then poured some melted butter on the popcorn, and the three of them walked back to the family room.

"Do you want to play checkers?" Jerry asked.

"Sure, where's the board?" Tess asked.

"Under the TV cabinet. Joe, get it out."

Joe crawled across the carpet and pulled the checkerboard out from under the TV.

"I get to go first since I got the board out," Joe whined.

"All right. Don't be such a baby." Jerry crammed another handful of buttery popcorn into his mouth.

173

"Ongwy don taktoo yong," he said through his stuffed mouth. After swallowing, Jerry said, "I'm going to wash this slimy butter off my hands while you guys play." Pushing himself to his feet, he ambled toward the kitchen.

Tess and Joe moved their pieces around the board and through the squares until Tess won. "Hey, you're bigger so you're supposed to let me win!" Joe whined. "Besides, my mom is paying you."

"She's paying me to baby-sit you, not to let you win," Tess said. "What's taking Jerry so long?"

"I'll go see." Joe stood up and headed for the kitchen.

Tess grabbed the remote control and flipped through the channels for a minute. She paused on an advertisement for "Miracle Cream, the beauty dream for skin so soft your man will beam."

Hmm, Tess thought, *my mom writes better ads than that. They should hire her, and they would sell more. Hey, maybe Erin and I could sell stuff. We would make way more money than baby-sitting, and I could still buy something nice for Mom.*

"Knock it off!"

A shout interrupted her thoughts, and she ran to the kitchen. As soon as she entered, a spray of water shot across the room, nailing her in the face. "You guys, turn that water off right now."

Jerry aimed one last squirt at Joe's face with the sink's nozzle attachment before twisting the cold water off. Tess headed toward him; he tried to escape her grasp and fell flat on the floor, slipping on a puddle.

"Ouch!" he bawled.

Joe laughed. "Serves you right; you started it!"

"Guys, guys." Tess tried to calm everyone down. "Are you okay?"

The boys nodded glumly, refusing to look at each other.

"Here, let's clean up." Ripping several sheets of paper towels off the rack, Tess handed the wad to Joe. "Start mopping."

Jerry smirked. Tess tore off more paper towels. "You, too," she said, handing the second wad to Jerry.

A few minutes later the kitchen looked tiptop again, and the boys watched a video until Mrs. Kim came home.

After Mrs. Kim paid her, Tess ran to her waiting family. "Thank goodness you're here!" Tess said to her dad as she climbed into the car. "That job is work! I'm happy to be leaving to go to the real circus, although it seems like one in there."

"Most jobs are work, Tess," Dad said with a smile. "What happened?"

"They had a water fight, and we had to mop up the whole kitchen. But I earned another fifteen dollars; so now I have thirty dollars."

"What are you going to do with it?" her mom asked as she twisted the rearview mirror toward herself to fix a contact.

"I can't see what's behind me," Tess's dad grumbled. He always grumbled when she took the mirror.

"Now, dear, I'm already done," she said, twisting the mirror back. "Well, Tess, what are you going to buy?"

"I don't know. I saw an ad today for some Miracle Cream."

"Miracle Cream! That's dumb," Tyler said. "I'd buy something cool, like Lizard Village or a Scotland Yard trench coat. It's not fair. Girls can baby-sit to make money, but boys can't do anything! Dad says I'm too young to mow lawns, and there's nothing else to do." He crossed his arms for emphasis.

"You have the rest of your life to work, Ty," their dad teased.

"And boys can baby-sit," Mrs. Thomas added.

"I didn't say I was going to buy Miracle Cream!" Tess interjected. "I was just going to tell Mom I thought she could write a better ad. This one was goofy."

"Thank you, Tess," said her mom. "I'll keep it in mind. Now, let's all help Dad look for a good parking spot." After five minutes spent circling the arena, she finally spied a spot, and Mr. Thomas pulled the car in.

"I'm so excited! I can hardly believe it! This is the best day of my life!" Tyler practically leaped out of the car and started to walk toward the arena door.

"Wait up, Ty," their dad said. "This is a busy street. We need to walk across together."

Once inside the arena, they climbed row after row of stairs until they reached their seats. "My dad would say we were two rows from heaven when we sat this high up," Mrs. Thomas joked.

Tess looked up. She wondered if heaven was that close. Sometimes she thought it was, but sometimes it seemed very far away.

Darkness fell across the room, and the circus started. Neon necklaces that had been hawked by the walking vendors flashed color strips here and there through the inky black. Men in tall hats stationed themselves around the crowd like the royal guard, steadying stacked trays of Sno-Kones and popcorn and peddling furry tigers at "exorbitant prices," according to Mr. Thomas. A roar swelled from the crowd as clown after painted clown paraded around the ring, followed by bejeweled elephants and exotic women. Tigers with shiny orange coats and saber-toothed grins leaped about the center ring.

The first act was the flying trapeze artists, some with safety ropes, some without. Their white sequined costumes reflected the strobe light, making the performers look like angels flitting through the air unaided. Soon after their act ended, the roar of metallic engines filled the great hall and was so loud Tess covered her ears. Thick exhaust fumes rose to their seats, clinging to the air around them as the daredevil motorcyclists entered the Globe of Death. Unbelievably, they circled one another again and again, three motorcycles riding at high speed inside a wire globe.

In awe, Tyler elbowed Tess. "Have you ever seen

anything so great?" He was so excited he forgot his British accent.

"Actually, Tyler, I think the whole circus is pretty cool," Tess whispered back. "I'm glad you wanted to come."

After an hour, intermission was announced, and the lights flashed on.

"Let's get a soda," Mr. Thomas suggested. The four of them began the long descent down to the snack-bar area. On the way Tyler discovered a booth selling mini Globes of Death and ran over to them, pulling his family along. Small motorcycles rode around the inside of the globe, a perfect replica of the show they had just seen.

"Can I get one? Please, please?" he asked.

Mom shook her head. "They're twelve dollars, Tyler. That's too much."

Dad nodded in agreement. "I don't mind paying for the tickets, but extras are your responsibility. Don't you have any allowance saved up?"

"Nah." Tyler shook his head, looking dejected. "I spent it."

As they started to walk away, Tess tugged on her mother's arm, stopping her. "Wait a second." Tess fumbled in her pocket until she pulled out two neatly folded bills, the ones Mrs. Kim had used to pay her a couple of hours before. "Here, Tyler, you can have this," she said.

"Are you serious?" Tyler stared at her with disbelief.

Tess nodded her head, then stuffed the bills into

his hand. "Quick, get one before they sell out."

"Thanks, Tess. You're the best sister in the whole world!" Tyler gave her a high-five then hopped over to the sales booth with his mother.

Mr. Thomas pulled Tess toward him, hugging her against his side as he did. "That was very generous, Tess. I know how hard you worked for that money."

"Yeah, well, it's okay," Tess said. She was happy she could use the money to buy something nice for her brother, even if she couldn't buy new earrings for her mom. And maybe her parents would notice how responsible she was acting, sharing and all. She and her dad slowly strolled toward the refreshment stand to order sodas before the show resumed.

Sandra Byrd

Chapter Eleven
Bull's-Eye

Tuesday, October 22

"How was the circus last night?" Erin called over the bathroom stall as she struggled to zip up the top Tess had brought for her to wear.

"It was totally fun. I liked the trapeze the best. Tyler liked the Globe of Death, and Mom liked the tigers. Dad said he liked the popcorn best, but he was joking. I think he liked the flame eaters. What size is this, anyway?" Tess sucked in her stomach and buttoned the jeans. She fluffed the shirt over her waistline and dug into the bottom of the brown bag for accessories.

"Doesn't it fit?" Erin asked. "This is great. I love beads. I didn't know you had a bead necklace."

"Yeah, my cousin sends me jewelry every year for Christmas. Sometimes it's good; sometimes it's not. Last year, she hit a winner."

"Back to the circus," Erin said. "They ate flames?"

"Yeah, it was weird. I've always been afraid of fire; so it was pretty scary just to watch."

The girls came out of the stalls at almost the same time. "Ta da!" Erin said, twirling so Tess could see the warm peach top, the beaded necklace, and the khaki pants. "What do you think?"

"It looks a lot better on you than on me," Tess said. "And what do you think about my wardrobe?" she teased.

"Great. I knew it was you!" Erin said admiringly. Tess wore a pair of Erin's black jeans and a kitten-soft, lightweight white sweater. "White isn't so good on me. But with your darker hair, it's just right."

Well, that's a first, Tess thought. *My hair is good for something!*

The bathroom door squeaked open, and Tess and Erin turned to see who was coming in. Colleen, Tess's one-time best friend, and her partner in crime, Lauren, strutted into the bathroom. Colleen stared coolly at Tess, then whispered something in Lauren's ear. Lauren looked back and laughed, then headed into a stall. Tess felt chilled and was glad Erin was there. Tess and Erin gathered their things into the brown paper sacks and were just ready to leave when Lauren came out to wash her hands. Lauren glared into the mirror with an "I'm great and you're bait" look.

"Hey, Lauren," Erin said.

"Yes?" Lauren answered, in a how-dare-you-talk-to-me voice.

"I'd take the toilet paper off of my backpack before I went into class, if I were you," Erin said. Then she and Tess headed toward the door. Tess sneaked a peek as she walked out and saw Lauren plucking two squares of wet toilet paper from the back of her pack.

Once in their classroom, Erin said, giggling, "Some things never change."

"It's true." Tess nodded in agreement. How could she ever have wanted to be like Colleen and Lauren? How could she have thought Colleen was her friend? After Colleen had burned Tess last month, she knew the truth. And now she had Erin, a true friend and a sister.

"Let's never be like that," Tess said.

"I agree," Erin answered. Tess took off her bracelet to swap with Erin, to seal the deal.

A few hours later, at lunch, Erin waved her hand in front of Tess to get her attention. "Yoo-hoo, are you here?"

"Yeah, yeah, I'm here."

"Isn't that great about Ms. M? I was so proud of my brave sister. You must have gotten all the courage genes!" Erin said.

"What's so brave about asking her?" Tess asked. "Do you think she will invite us to the wedding?"

"The whole class? I don't know. Maybe they wouldn't all want to go. Like Joann, for instance." Erin stood up. "Come on. Let's go outside."

Tess gladly agreed. They walked past the boys' table, and Tess noticed Erin blush as she glanced at Scott Shearin. Hmm, she would have to ask Erin about that later.

The weather was cooler now, and a thoughtful

breeze blew out summer, ushering in the desert fall. A few leaves, wet from the sprinklers, stuck to the playground fence like soggy Wheaties to the side of a cereal bowl. Autumn in Arizona was like a second spring, and people spent more time outside.

The two girls walked to a corner of the school and sat down against the outer brick wall. Erin crossed one leg over the other.

"Remember when you asked me the other day what sin was? Well, I had a chance to talk with my Sunday school teacher about it and she reminded me of this verse." Erin pulled out a piece of notebook paper.

Tess read, "'If we say that we have no sin, we are fooling ourselves, and the truth is not in us. But if we confess our sins, he will forgive our sins. We can trust God. He does what is right. He will make us clean from all the wrongs we have done'—1 John 1:8-9."

Erin chewed on her pencil before taking the piece of paper back from Tess. "Even little wrongs."

Tess smoothed out the paper and picked at the ragged edges. "I was wrong with those earrings."

"It's okay. God knows we make mistakes. That's why it's so great that as soon as we tell him we're sorry, he forgives us. So we don't have to walk around feeling bad or guilty all the time."

"So, is that what being a Christian is?"

"What do you mean?"

"Just memorizing the Bible and doing what it says?"

"No, silly." Erin punched Tess's arm. "You ask his forgiveness for your sins, and you trust him to take charge of your life because He loves you and He knows everything. And then you're friends, too."

Tess sat quietly, thinking about how she had tried to blame God at the mall for not finding the earrings. She guessed that was missing the mark, too. "Still, I don't think there's anything so great about me that God would want me."

"God thinks you're great, Tess, and so do I. You're the only sister I've ever had."

"Thanks. But I don't want to talk about this anymore, okay? We only have a few minutes left before class. Let's go on the bars." Tess stuffed the paper into her jeans pocket, and they joined some of the girls from their class in a chasing game.

Chapter Twelve
911

Wednesday, October 23

Tess walked up to her house, flipped open the mailbox at the end of her driveway, and sifted through the mail. "Why do I do this? There's never anything for me."

She shuffled through the catalogs and bills and looked at contests and coupons for carpet cleaning. Then a curious pink envelope caught her eye. It was addressed to: Tess Thomas. The return address was: You'll Never Guess, 1000 Secrets Lane, Sistersville, AZ.

"Who could this be from?" she wondered, ripping open the envelope.

Tess slipped a pretty pink note card from the envelope and read, "Roses are red, but my sister is blue. I want you to know that I'm thinking of you." Tess smiled and put the card back into the envelope. What a good friend.

She set her backpack on the floor and hummed to herself as she pulled a package of chicken pieces out of the refrigerator. This, she thought, would be the ultimate gift to her mother during her week of trying to do really wonderful things. Her mom would forgive her for the earrings for sure now. Poking her fingernail through the plastic wrapping, she heard a little "pop" as the wrap snapped.

"Now, what am I supposed to dip this stuff into?" Thumbing through her mom's big cookbook, she found a recipe for fried chicken and read, "Put flour, salt, and pepper in a medium-sized bowl. Dip chicken pieces in raw egg then dredge in flour mix. Fry pieces until golden brown."

Molly Thomas loved fried chicken, and Tess wanted to make sure she prepared it just right for her mother. Tess had never actually fried anything before, but it couldn't be too hard. After dipping the chicken in the egg and then the flour, she put the pieces in a pan with a large amount of oil. Then Tess washed her hands, and taking a head of lettuce and several tomatoes out of the refrigerator, she turned her attention to the salad.

"What are you doing?" Tyler and Big Al walked into the kitchen.

"Making dinner."

"Blimey. Does Mom know?"

"No, silly. It's a surprise. She's going to be back from the dentist's office in a few minutes, and I wanted to have this done so she could relax."

Big Al opened his mouth, propelling a huge belch from the yawning hole. Suddenly the smell of rotten hot dogs filled the room.

"That was totally disgusting. You guys get out of here."

"Come on, Tyler. Let's go throw the ball." Laughing, the two of them headed out to the front yard to toss a baseball around. Tess turned back to the salad.

Funny, that burp must have been worse than she had thought because now it smelled smoky. Her nose twitched as the awful smell grew stronger. Tess twirled around and saw swirls of black smoke rising from the frying pan. Splatters of oil popped out of the pan onto the stove-top, and she could see the oil smoking more and more.

"Oh, no. Now what?" She grasped the panhandle but recoiled as the heat burned her hand. "Where is the potholder?" She searched frantically as the smoke grew thicker. The splattering reached the floor now. Still unable to locate the potholders, she grabbed a dishtowel and grabbed the handle again.

As she picked up the pan, the towel rested a moment too long on the heating element. Suddenly the entire towel caught fire, racing up to Tess's hand. "Ouch, ouch, ouch!" she cried, throwing the burning towel. Almost instantly the small garbage can in which the towel landed caught fire. "What should I do?" she cried aloud. Running to the telephone she quickly dialed 911.

"911. Fire, police, or ambulance?" The operator spoke in a too-calm voice.

"Please help. I've started my house on fire!" Tess shouted into the receiver.

"Is anyone else in the house?"

"No, my brother and his friend are outside.

Everyone else is gone. Please get someone here quickly!" Tess screamed.

"Okay, miss, your address popped up on our screen; someone is on the way. Go out of the house to flag down the fire trucks." Tess tried to hang up the phone, but her hands were shaking so hard she dropped the receiver and flew out the door.

Her voice trembled as she screamed, "Tyler!"

Tyler and Big Al took one look at her face and ran to her side. "What's the matter?" Tyler asked.

"The house is on fire; the house is on fire!" Tess cried.

"What do you mean?" Big Al asked.

"It's on fire! Please, God, let the fire trucks get here." In a moment the sad wail of sirens could be heard several streets away.

Tyler's eyes grew as big as an owl's. "Are you okay? What happened? Boy, are you going to be in trouble."

Tess knew the fire trucks were almost there, but the waiting seemed unbearable. Suddenly, the trucks turned the corner, and the three kids flailed their arms wildly to get the firefighters' attention. Two big trucks, a pumper truck and a hook and ladder, pulled up. A large man in yellow and gray reflective turn-out gear jumped off the truck and ran up to Tess while two other firefighters hauled a hose toward the house.

"Is anyone in the house, miss?" he asked in a kind voice.

"No, no, everyone's out here."

"Where are your parents?"

"My dad is at work, and my mom is at the dentist. She'll be back soon." At that thought, Tess started to cry again.

"Don't worry, young lady. We'll take care of everything." The firefighter sent the three of them to wait by the curb while he joined his partners at the front of the house. He sent someone over to look at Tess's hand.

"This is a nasty burn, miss. You need to get this taken care of right away. Here, wrap this cold pack around it. It will lessen the pain for about half an hour. By then, you should have some medical treatment." The firefighter wrapped a cool, blue quilted bandage with icy water between its layers around Tess's hand. He was right; it did soothe the throbbing hand a little bit. But it still hurt, bad. Where was Mom?

A few minutes later her car came barreling down the street. It screeched to a halt in front of the house. Tess could read the fear in her mother's face as she viewed the fire trucks, then the relief as she saw the three of them out front.

"What's going on? Is everyone okay?" she asked Tess.

"Mom, I'm so sorry. I wanted to make you fried chicken, and I grabbed the pan with a dishtowel, but it caught on fire. The next thing I knew the garbage can was on fire; so I called 911."

Tess started to cry all over again. Tyler and Big Al stood dumbfounded, watching the firefighters.

191

Tess's mom hugged her. A few minutes later the captain signaled for Mrs. Thomas to come over.

Tess waited by the curb, but she could hear him. "Everything is okay. There is minor damage to one wall, and the curtains are burned. It's mostly cosmetic, nothing unsafe, but it will be a shock at first. Your daughter's hand could use some medical attention. I don't think it's too bad. I didn't want to call an ambulance and scare her further. A doctor should see her, though."

"Thank you," her mom said. "I'll take her to the emergency room right away."

The firefighters packed up their gear, and the two trucks rolled down the street back to the firehouse. Tess's mom walked slowly back to her. "My goodness, my goodness, whatever will we tell Jim?" she muttered to herself. After glancing at Tess's face, she added, "Don't worry, honey. Accidents happen. Let's go to the emergency room to take care of your hand. We'll talk about this later." She went into the house to survey the damage and to call her husband. A minute later she came back out to the front yard.

Tess sobbed as she climbed into the car, but she slowly calmed down. "Let's take Al home on the way," her mother suggested. Tyler nodded his head, and the two boys got into the car. Mrs. Thomas looked at Tess's throbbing red skin, adjusted the cool wrap, and stepped on the gas. Tess stared out the window the whole way to the hospital, jiggling her hand up and down in her lap to distract her from the pain.

Chapter Thirteen
Making Things Right

Wednesday Evening, October 23

"Wait in here, please. The doctor will be just a minute." The nurse pulled the door shut, leaving Tess and her mother alone in the room. Tyler had decided to wait at Big Al's until Mr. Thomas could pick him up.

"Tell me what happened, Tess," her mom said gently.

"Just what I said, Mom. I wanted to make some fried chicken for you. You know, to do something really nice like I've been trying to do all week. I thought if I made your favorite dinner, then you could relax when you got home, and you would totally forgive me for losing your earrings. Only the oil started to smoke, and when I tried to take the pan off the stove, the towel caught fire. When it burned my hand, I threw the towel, and it landed in the garbage can. I called 911 and ran outside." Tess sat quietly.

"I know it was an accident. I appreciate that you were trying to do something nice for me, Tess. But I told you the other day, you don't have to do anything else to make up for the lost earrings. I forgive you; I understand that people make mistakes. 'Forgive' means I am 'giving' you the gift of forgetting the wrong. You don't earn it; it's a gift. That's what the 'give' part of the word means. So please don't do anything else to try to make it up to me." Her eyes twinkled. "Especially frying chicken!"

"Don't worry about that! I'm never cooking again, or at least not for a few years!" Tess promised. The door swung open.

"Let's see that hand, young lady," the doctor said as she entered the room. She shook hands with Tess's mom. "I'm Dr. Norton." Gently turning Tess's hand and lower arm, the doctor examined the burn. "I don't think it's too serious. Let's put some medicated ointment on it and wrap it in gauze." She sprayed Tess's skin with a cool mist. "That's to deaden the pain while I spread the cream." Then she spread some thick white cream on the burned area and rewrapped it in a fresh bandage.

"You should stay home from school for a couple of days to avoid infections or bumping the healing tissue. Have your regular doctor check it on Friday. What's your doctor's name? I'll have my nurse call to make the appointment for you."

"I'll come with you so we can find a time that will work for both of us," her mom said. "Will you be okay?" she asked Tess.

"Yes, Mom, nothing to burn down in here," Tess joked. "And the skin does feel better with that stuff on it." For the first time since she had burned her hand, Tess could move it without too much pain.

Dr. Norton and her mother left the room, and Tess looked around her. A blood pressure machine with its black air hoses was screwed into the wall. A scary-looking cabinet had a sign attached to it that read "Oxygen Tent." Kicking her feet against the back of the table she sat on, Tess examined the chart over the sink. "The Skeletal System," it read. It was more detailed than the skeleton in the mall, with lots of blue and red veins woven alongside pink muscles. Not a Halloween decoration, but a skeleton nonetheless.

"God, do you see my heart? If you can see my heart, you know I meant to do something good this time."

The door swung open again, and the nurse came in with some information on caring for burns. Then she sent Tess out to the waiting room. "Your mom is waiting for you. I gave her the instructions," the nurse said.

"Thank you," Tess said.

Mrs. Thomas picked up her purse and put her arm around Tess, guiding her to the car in the dusky evening light. Two squirrels scurried through the parking lot, seeking walnuts under the trees. Tess smiled at their chatter, and her mom smiled, too.

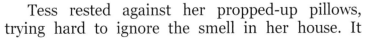

Tess rested against her propped-up pillows, trying hard to ignore the smell in her house. It reminded her of a campfire that had been doused.

"Hello?"

"Hi, this is Tess."

"I know who you are, silly. How are you?"

"Not so good, actually," Tess said. "I started my house on fire and had to go to the hospital."

"What?!" Erin shouted into the phone. "Are you okay?"

"Yeah, I got a little burned, but I'm okay, and so is everyone else. The house isn't even too bad, if you ignore the smell. It's a long story; I'll tell you more later. What I really wanted to know is if you could bring my assignments to my house tomorrow. I have to stay home for two days until the bandages get changed on my hand."

"Sure, Tess. I'm sorry you'll miss school tomorrow. We're going to read our stories and have popcorn and stuff."

"I know," lamented Tess. "But there's nothing I can do about it. Hey, thanks for the card! I really loved it."

"You're welcome. I hope it made you feel better. Plus, I always like to get mail."

"Me, too," Tess said, "and I never do." After a quiet moment she continued, "I saw a skeleton at the hospital."

"A skeleton?" Erin asked.

"Yeah. And I was wondering, do you think God loves me enough to forgive me? My mom said she forgives me, but she's my mom."

"Yes, Tess, he does. I wish you could hear my

story tomorrow. I heard it last Sunday and liked it so much I chose it for my project."

"Yeah, well, maybe you can bring it over when you bring my other homework." A few seconds passed in silence. "I'd better go. My hand hurts."

"Okay. Bye, Tess," Erin said.

Tess gently hung up the phone then walked to her closet. Picking up the white jeans she wore yesterday, she pulled out the pocket, searching for the piece of paper Erin had given her. She laughed. Last time she was looking in these pockets it was for the earrings. She hoped the paper wasn't lost. She found it and opened it up.

"God makes people right with himself through their faith in Jesus Christ," she read. Hmm. Not from doing good stuff all the time, or being skinny or popular or smart. Or never making mistakes. Like setting a house on fire or ripping off your mom's earrings.

After clicking off her light, she folded up the piece of paper and stared out her window. Mr. and Mrs. Cricket were there, chirping cheerfully. Goldy swam round and round her slimy bowl, getting in her exercise.

"Tomorrow," Tess promised herself, "I'll clean off the slime." She snuggled down in her bed and tried to sleep.

Sandra Byrd

Chapter Fourteen
Twenty-One Ponies

Thursday Night, October 24

"Erin's here," Tyler shouted as he knocked on Tess's bedroom door.

"Will you send her in?"

"Okay"

A few seconds later Erin appeared at Tess's doorway. "Hi. How are you feeling?"

"Okay. My hand feels much better today."

"Could I see where the fire was?"

"Sure." Tess closed her book and hopped off her bed. She slipped her feet into her warm wool slippers and adjusted her sweatshirt. "Come on. I'll tell you all about it on the way."

"Man, this still looks pretty ugly," Erin said.

"I know. My mom is going to buy some new curtains, and my dad is going to paint the wall. I think it will look okay then."

A few minutes later, after they had walked back down the hall into Tess's room, she said, "How was school today?"

"Totally fun. I'm sorry you had to miss it. Ms. M.

199

made popcorn and brought chocolate and fruit punch."

Tess smiled. Leave it to Erin to tell her about the food first. "How did the stories go?"

"Great. They were pretty good. I can't believe how well some of those guys can write. People you would never guess, like Angela and Steven."

"How did yours go?" Tess asked.

"Fine. Everyone liked my story, too. I told them it was a missionary story but didn't say the whole comparison. I wrote it on the bottom of the page, though, so you can read it."

"What do you mean, the whole comparison?"

"You'll see when you read it," Erin said. "Hey, before I forget, here are your assignments." She dumped a pile of books onto Tess's bed and handed her a folder full of papers. "Ms. M. wrote out all the instructions for both today and tomorrow. I told her you would be back Monday, right?" Erin asked.

"Yep, that's right. Hey, what's that?" Pulling a large piece of orange construction paper from the stack, Tess opened it up to its full size.

"We made you a card. Everyone signed it."

Tess smiled, looking it over. "Was this your idea?"

"No, um, actually..." Erin seemed embarrassed. "Believe it or not, it was Joann's."

Joann! Tess never would have guessed.

Everyone had written something or drawn smiley faces or hearts. Erin signed it, "Your Secret Sister" and someone else had scribbled, "What?" next to that. Tess opened her desk drawer and pulled out a roll of Scotch tape, then stuck the card to her wall.

"Thanks for bringing everything over, Erin." Tess hugged her.

"No problem. It's what any sister would do. I'll miss you tomorrow. Oh, here are your clothes. My mom was, um, a little upset that we changed clothes at school. She thought maybe we should only switch clothes at home from now on."

"Okay. Sounds fine."

"Yeah, I'd better go. My dad is waiting." Erin beamed. "He took the night off."

"Great. I'll call you tomorrow night to find out what happened in class."

After Erin left, Tess shut the door and kicked off her slippers. She sifted through the stack on her bed, opening the manila envelope marked "Twenty-One Ponies." *This must be Erin's story.* She pulled the sheets of paper from the envelope and settled back on her bed to read.

Twenty-One Ponies

Long, long ago on the dusty prairie of the wild west, a tribe of native Americans lived, a large tribe with many traditions and customs. The old people of this tribe told the stories of their past so the young people would never forget. One particularly old woman, named Rock by the Bank, told the best stories. Because she had only three teeth you had to listen closely to understand her words. Her favorite story went like this:

One year the most eligible young brave in the village grew to be the age that men are when they choose a bride. Each day he sat outside his tent, watching the young women of the tribe. One girl was the most beautiful. Her long black braids hung down her back, reflecting the summer light. Her skin was as smooth as a stone on the bottom of a quick-moving stream. Another girl was wise. She taught the others how to weave and how to braid detailed patterns. Another girl knew the best places to find tasty berries and roots. Whoever married this girl would certainly eat well. None of these women stirred his heart.

One day his attention was drawn to a shy young woman who normally stood to the side of the others. This young woman, named Forget Me Not, was not particularly beautiful nor did she weave beautiful bracelets or headbands. The first morning he observed her she brushed the mud off the moccasins of the others who had kicked them off in their haste to get to the river. That same afternoon she comforted the crying baby of a new mother, enabling the mother to prepare the evening meal. Although

Forget Me Not's singing voice was not particularly good, the brave noticed that, when the woman laughed, all those around her laughed, too. Her joy was contagious. He decided he wanted that joy in his household.

According to the custom of his people, he approached the girl's father. "I would like your daughter's hand in marriage," he said. "What will her bride-price be?"

"This one is not beautiful, nor does she know where to find hidden fruit. I think one pony will be enough," the father answered.

The brave and the father shook hands, and the young man agreed to come back the next week to claim his bride. That night he peeked outside as the village girls giggled. "One pony isn't much," one said. "Of course, Forget Me Not isn't a valuable bride."

"That's true," another one chimed in. "My betrothed promised three horses for me!"

The brave closed his teepee to think. The next morning, he came to me, Rock by the Bank, and asked, "What is the biggest dowry paid by any man in the history of our tribe?"

I told him, "Legend says that twenty ponies were paid for Prairie Thorn's hand

in marriage in my grandmother's years."
The brave thanked me, then went home.

That week he rounded up his
seventeen horses, all but his favorite. He
traded some fine beaten silver to another
brave for two more ponies and a large
sack of grain for another. Finally, he
walked out to where his horses stood. His
favorite, the one he had raised since birth,
stood outside the crowd.

This pony was special, unblemished,
unbroken to the ways of the world. The
brave loved this pony more than anything
else in the world; it was more valuable to
him than all his other possessions
combined. After kissing the pony's coat,
he led him with all the others to his new
father-in-law's house. As the ponies beat
a path to the door, the entire village
gathered around, wondering why there
was a stampede.

"Here I am," the brave called. "Come to
collect my bride."

The father-in-law answered, "But I
said one pony was enough."

"No," said the brave. "My bride is
worth more than all others in the entire
history of our tribe. Here are twenty-one
ponies, including my favorite."

Forget Me Not walked out of the tent
to join her new husband, holding her

head high before all those who had made fun of her. For the rest of her life she knew her husband prized her enough to give up all he had for her, not for what she had to offer, but because she herself was loved.

Tess noticed that Erin had scribbled at the bottom of the page, "So you see, Tess, this is really the story about God, the brave, and his love for his bride, you. He gave everything he had for you, including that which he loves the most, Jesus. Not because you do anything great, but because he loves you exactly as you are. That's why he will forgive you, and you can trust him with your whole life and be his friend forever. Isn't this a neat story? I heard it last Sunday night."

Tess walked into the silent kitchen and squeaked open the patio door. The evening was light on her skin, the breeze soothing her as it lifted up her hair. The pool cleaner wandered on its nightly rounds. As she watched the cleaner, Tess wiped two small tears off her cheek and reclined in a worn-out woven lawn chair and looked up toward heaven. "Yes, God, I understand," she whispered. "You do want me and love me. I'm sorry for taking the earrings and then blaming you. And for all the other times I made mistakes, big and small." She lay there for another minute.

"I don't know if I said everything right, or what I'm supposed to do after this. Please forgive me. I want things to be right between us. I don't really know what to do next, though, so you'll have to tell me. I'd like us to be friends."

She didn't hear a voice, but almost immediately she felt peace and joy wrap around her like the fuzzy pink blanket that Baby Dimples, her doll, snuggled in. Even though the night was dark and starry, Tess felt warm, as if she had climbed out of a chilly pool into the strong summer sunshine. In some way, Tess felt as if she had been underwater for a long time and only now could she deeply draw in some fresh air and really breathe.

Chapter Fifteen
Real Sisters

Friday, October 25

"Isn't it great how fast my hand is healing?" Tess asked. "I'm glad I can go to school Monday. I want to be there when we blow the volcano."

"Yes, honey, it really is great." Her dad pulled the car into the driveway. "Mom will be pleased to see the bandages are off." He stopped the motor, and they got out of the car. "I'm going to do a little work in the garage. Why don't you go tell Mom you're home?"

"Okay." Tess walked into the kitchen. "Here I am. No bandages! Dr. Irvine says my hand looks good."

"I'm glad," said her mother. "Why don't you help me make some dinner?"

Her mom's face sported a huge smile. She must have had a fantastic day. But why was she flinging her hair around? Every time she turned around, her hair swung away from the sides of her face. Weird. Tess turned back to the sink.

"Notice anything?" asked her mom.

"Uh, let's see." Tess stared. Not new clothes or

shoes. "New makeup?" she guessed hopefully.

"No, silly, look!" She swept back her hair again. There, like twin twinkling stars, were the diamond wedding earrings, one clinging for dear life to each ear.

"Mom! Where did they come from?" The carrot scraper dropped in the sink as Tess rushed over to hug her mother. "Oh, Mom, I'm so happy!"

"Me, too, honey. While you and Dad were at the doctor's office, Erin stopped by with these. I guess the church landscaper found them in the bushes next to the driveway, where you must have dropped them. When he pruned the bushes, they practically called out to him. After he took them to the church office, the secretary called Erin's mom, who picked them up. She and Erin rushed right over here. Oh, Tess," she said, "isn't this wonderful?"

"Yeah, it's been a great week! I'm going to go call Erin and thank her." Skipping out of the kitchen, Tess headed to her room. She picked up the phone to dial, then set it down.

"God, thank you for the earrings. You got them back for me after all!" Grabbing the phone again, she dialed Erin's number.

"Hello?"

"Great job!" Tess shouted into the phone. "I am so excited I can barely even talk!"

"I know. I couldn't believe it myself! My mom and I practically laughed the whole way to pick them up."

"Guess what else?" Tess asked.

"What?"

"I loved your story. And I understood it!"

"That's great! This is one of the best days of my life. I can't believe it!"

"Why not?"

"I don't know. It seems so fantastic. God answered my prayer and yours, too. It's too dreamy to be true. But it is true! Do you know what else?" Erin asked.

"What?"

"Well, now we're not just Secret Sisters, we're real sisters, spiritual sisters."

"What does that mean?"

"Well, Christians call other Christians their sisters and brothers. So now you're really my sister."

"Does that mean Tom is my brother?" Tess giggled. "I kind of hope not!"

"Ha! Hey, what did your mom and dad say?"

The room was silent for what seemed like ten minutes, although it was probably less than one. "Tess? Are you still there?"

"Yes."

"Well, what do your mom and dad think?"

"I haven't told them yet. I guess I will later."

"Oh. Okay. I'd better go, I hear my mom calling us for dinner. We can talk more tomorrow, all right?"

"Okay, Sis. See you later." Tess hung up the phone and sat heavily on her bed. She had forgotten about telling her parents. Somehow she thought her mom wouldn't mind, but she knew dad wasn't into religion. This wasn't just religion, but would he see it that way? Maybe she would tell them next week, after she had thought about a good way to say it.

She glanced at the orange card on her wall, reminding her how much the class cared for her. On the spur of the moment, she pulled out her top desk drawer and grabbed a snapshot of her and Erin riding horses at Erin's party last month. She taped it to the wall next to the card.

"I hope we're Secret Sisters forever," she whispered, heading back to the kitchen.

 Have More Fun!!

Everyone likes to get mail, and your secret sister is no exception! Putting together a special correspondence file makes it easy for you to surprise her with mail.
You need:

    1 folder with pockets on each inside flap
    4 sheets of paper or blank cards
    4 envelopes
    Stickers
    4 stamps

Pick a time of the week, for example, Sunday night, to write your sister a little letter. It can be a rhyming poem or a coded message or just a few words about how exceptional she is. Decorate it with your stickers and markers or pretty hole punchers if you like. Fold it and stamp it and stick it into your mailbox before you go to bed. Your sis will get a Tuesday surprise in the real mail - not email - and might even write you back!

Sandra Byrd

Love the Secret Sisters books? Please leave a review so other girls will read the books, and find their own Secret Sisters, too!!

Look for the other titles in Sandra Byrd's Secret Sisters Series!

Secret Sisters #2: Accidental Angel

Star Light: Tess's mother becomes seriously ill, and Tess's new faith is tested. Can she trust God with the big things as well as the small?

Accidental Angel: Tess and Erin have great plans for their craft-fair earnings. But after their first big fight will they still want to spend it together? And how does Tess become the "accidental" angel?

Secret Sisters #3: Double Dare

Double Dare: A game of "truth or dare" leaves Tess feeling like she doesn't measure up. Will making the gymnastics team prove she can excel?

War Paint: Tess must choose between running for Miss Coronado and entering the school mural-painting contest with Erin. There are big opportunities—and a big blowout with the Coronado Club.

Secret Sisters #4: Backdoor Bridesmaid

Holiday Hero: This could be the best Spring Break ever—or the worst Tess's brother, Tyler, is saved from disaster, but can the sisters rescue themselves from even bigger problems?

Backdoor Bridesmaid: Ms. Martinez is the most beautiful bride in the world, and the sisters are there to help her get married. When trouble strikes her honeymoon plans, Tess and Erin must find a way to help save them.

Secret Sisters #5: Camp Cowgirl

First Place: The Coronado Club insists Tess won't be able to hike across the Grand Canyon and plans to tell the whole sixth grade about it at Outdoor School. Tess looks confident but worries in silence, not wanting to share the secret that could lead to disaster.

Camp Cowgirl: The Secret Sisters are ready for an awesome summer camp at a Tucson horse ranch, until something—and someone—interferes. What happens if your best friend wants other friends, and you're not sure, but you might too?

Secret Sisters #6: Picture Perfect

Picture Perfect: Tess and Erin sign up for modeling school, but will they be able to go? Could they ever get any modeling assignments? Along the way the Secret Sisters find out that things aren't always just as they seem, a fact confirmed when Tess's mother has her baby.

Indian Summer: When Tess and Erin sign up to go on their first mission trip—to the Navajo reservation—they plan to teach Vacation Bible School. What do a young Navajo girl and Tess have in common? In the end Tess has to make some of the most important choices in her new Christian life.

Hidden Diary Series

Lucy is dreading another summer on the island away from her friends while her father works on his research project. Then she stumbles upon a letter from 1932 that gives mysterious clues about a hidden diary and how to find it. Along the way Lucy finds trouble, adventure, excitement, and a new best friend.

In four, action-packed, heart-touching volumes, Lucy and Serena track down the clues offered in an old diary. When they challenge one another to a diary dare, the risks and rewards only get bigger.

Each volume includes everything tweens want in a book: fun, friends, family, faith and a fast-pace. Go ahead - give them a try!

www.sandrabyrd.com